~~~~~~~~~~~~~~~~~~~

PURRFECT
CRIME

~~~~~~~~~~~~~~~~~~~

A Seacastle Christmas
Mystery Novella

PJ Skinner

ISBN 978-1-913224-54-7

Parkin Press

INDEPENDENT PUBLISHER

Discover other titles by PJ Skinner

The Seacastle Mysteries

Deadly Return (Seacastle Mysteries Book 1)

Eternal Forest (Seacastle Mysteries Book 2)

Fatal Tribute (Seacastle Mysteries Book 3)

Toxic Vows (Seacastle Mysteries Book 4)

Mortal Vintage (Seacastle Mysteries Book 5)

Last Orders (Seacastle Mysteries Book 6)

Grave Reality (Seacastle Mysteries Book 7)

Purrfect Crime (A Christmas Mystery novella)

Mortal Mission A Mars Murder Mystery written as Pip Skinner

Green Family Saga (written as Kate Foley)
Rebel Green (Book 1)
Africa Green (Book 2)
Fighting Green (Book 3)

The Sam Harris Adventure Series (written as PJ Skinner)

Fool's Gold (Book 1)

Hitler's Finger (Book 2)

The Star of Simbako (Book 3)

The Pink Elephants (Book 4)

The Bonita Protocol (Book 5)

Digging Deeper (Book 6)

Concrete Jungle (Book 7)

Sam Harris Adventure Box Set Book 2-4

Sam Harris Adventure Box Set Book 5-7

Sam Harris Adventure Box Set Books 2-7

Also available as AI narrated audiobooks on YouTube and from my website

Go to the PJ Skinner website for more info and to purchase paperbacks and audiobooks directly from the author: https://www.pjskinner.com

Dedicated to the Beta, ARC and Proof readers who have helped make this series a success.

You are special people

Chapter 1

If you have a cat, you'll know. They don't follow instructions. Hades, our rescue cat, delighted in thumbing his nose at me from the first day I discovered him trapped in a Lloyd Loom laundry basket in the empty house next door. He loved everybody except me, rubbing himself up against complete strangers and gloating as I fumed. He purred extra loud when he sat on a lap within hearing distance of me. A right royal ratbag. I had no idea why he singled me out for the cold shoulder. Perhaps he blamed me for his incarceration, as I was the one who let him out. Did he realise I paid for his ludicrously expensive cat food? Who knows what cats are thinking?

The shrill tone of the alarm on my phone made me jump and spill my tea. How had it got so late without me noticing? I had to leave immediately, or I would miss my appointment with the bank. My heart hammered against my ribs as I threw on my coat and patted the pockets. As I opened the front door, I felt Hades slip past me onto the pavement, which he had never done before. It hadn't occurred to me he would even try. He paused at the neighbouring house's doorstep, gazing up at the handle. I knew I should grab him, but I had only picked him up once after he saved me from an attack and we were both petrified. He dealt out a nasty scratch if I tried to take liberties with him. I tried not to panic and use a reasonable tone of voice.

'Hades, come here.'

He raised a metaphorical eyebrow at me and walked out into the middle of the street. He sat down and cleaned his fur as I inched closer to him. I leapt towards him, but he sidestepped me with the ease of Billy Whizz and sat down again just out of my reach. I checked my watch and wished I hadn't. I couldn't leave Hades outside. He had no experience of cars. He would get run over. A trickle of sweat ran down my back.

'Hades, I'm going to kill you.'

I could almost hear him gloating. Then, as suddenly as he had exited, he entered the house again of his own accord, his tail high in the air with triumph. I swore under my breath and shut the front door behind him. I trotted to my car and got in, taking a couple of deep breaths to slow my heart rate. The last thing I needed was to arrive at the bank flushed and sweaty, when I wanted to project an image of a competent business woman who ran a soon to be profitable business. My finances had suffered because of a droopy economy, but I felt confident of getting ahead again with successful December Christmas sales. The added expense of helping my stepson, Mouse, (George's son from his first marriage – it's complicated), at university had also put more pressure on my account. To my relief, the bank manager recognised me from "Uncovering the Truth". The television series had been my get-out-of-jail-free card for years. I had worked there as an investigative journalist and people still remembered me from my fleeting appearances on television every Sunday night. She seemed more interested in gleaning gossip about the show and its stars than questioning me about the likelihood of me paying back my overdraft.

I left the bank with a spring in my step and an extension to my loan, having signed an autograph for the bank manager's mother. I walked back down the High Street, admiring the elaborately decorated windows of many shops. Most of them had only recently organised themselves into these displays, a fact I appreciated. I love Christmas, but it seems to start earlier every year. I had entered a stationery shop to buy a new notebook months before the festive season and had been confronted by rows of jovial snowmen on Christmas cards. Honestly, it took me months to recover. However, as the actual week of Noel approached, I couldn't wait for the nativity, the tree, the decorations, the food — well everything really. Did I mention the chocolate reindeer?

Unfortunately, the chance of me getting any actual presents was remote. My ex-husband DI George Carter liked to receive them, but always had an excuse for not buying me anything, usually a murder case, or cigarette smugglers keeping him busy all hours of the day and night. George had moved on to new pastures, weirdly, my older sister Helen, but we were both happier as a result. While George and I were married, he used to rely on me for insights into his murder cases. After our divorce, he did not appreciate my input, but somehow, we seemed to cooperate more than he'd like to admit. We all got along most of the time, despite Helen's older sister habit of pointing out my shortcomings. Her condescending remarks about my cluttered home and overgrown garden were only slightly mitigated by her offer to cook Christmas lunch at my house.

As much as I dreaded Helen taking over my kitchen, it would give me more time to concentrate on Second Home, my vintage furniture and knick-knack business in this peak sales time. Christmas purchases were responsible for much of my annual profit at my shop, but I found it hard to maintain my seasonal cheer. A constant stream of browsers had picked up items and put them down again without buying throughout the run up to Christmas. I guessed they were doing their pre-Christmas perusal of possible gifts. I longed to put up a notice saying 'When it's gone, it's gone', because some people didn't understand the concept of a vintage shop. Either they thought my prices were too high, because they had seen something similar in the Oxfam charity shop for two quid, or they asked me when I would restock the vinyl stools which I had the week before.

'You sold the Habitat lamp? But I wanted it for my aunt.'

It's hard to remain sanguine when you are asked the same questions again and again, or people are just plain rude. A last-minute rush seemed inevitable with ensuing disappointment for them and more stress for me.

At least I had plenty of stock in the correct price range for bargain hunters when they eventually loosened their purse strings. My boyfriend and business partner Harry Fletcher and I did house clearances together, and we had recently hit the jackpot when we were asked to empty an old lamp shop. We found several beautiful anglepoise lamps and boxes of silk lampshades of many hues in the storeroom. They had been hidden from the light for forty years, so still looked brand new and had vibrant colours. I snaffled a couple for the Grotty Hovel, the small, terraced house where I lived with Harry and Mouse. Harry had recently moved in with me and we were as happy as two bugs in a rug. Our precarious finances had been shored up by running one household instead of two, but I always bought a lottery ticket, just in case.

As I entered Second Home, the old-fashioned bell on the door clanged a welcome and I stepped into my favourite shop. Vintage goodies filled the place from top to bottom, from the glass fisherman's floats hanging in nets from ceiling hooks, to the boxes of random treasures shoved under Formica tables for storage. The latter were artifices planted for people who love to rummage for a bargain. I knew exactly what each box contained, but for clients, the thrill of finding their hearts' desire could not be calculated in money. My friend, Roz Murray, manned the till in my absence, standing behind a counter salvaged from the old Italian café across the street. Tall, with a mop of fair curly hair which often changed colour, she wore her heart on her sleeve and wafty mermaid dresses in tulle and lace. Gossip was her superpower. She had an antenna like Jodrell Bank for any hint of scandal or juicy rumour. She often spent days out at sea with her husband Ed, fishing for scallops and prawns and crabs and lobsters, which they sold to restaurants around town.

'How did it go at the bank?' she said. 'Are you still solvent?'

'For now. We need a Christmas rush to refloat the boat.'

'Coffee?'

'Yes, please.'

She disappeared upstairs to the Vintage Café, the second part of my business, which had kept finances going when the shop did not. The hiss of the Gaggia soothed my worries, as I waited for my latte. The meeting with the bank manager had gone much better than I had expected, and a wave of optimism swept over me. It would all work out in the end. It always did.

Chapter 2

I returned from Second Home in a good mood, having sold a pair of Italian vases I'd displayed for several months. They were made by Giulianelli, a famous designer and worth a lot more than I charged for them. Unfortunately, his ornate designs had fallen out of fashion and his price had followed. I had picked them up in the clearance of a flat, which turned out to be owned by the former proprietors of the café across the street, the Bonettis. They had retired and moved back to Italy, leaving many of their treasures behind. In recent months, our friends, Rohan Patel and Kieron Murphy, had opened Surfusion, a high-end restaurant in the Bonettis' empty café, decorating it with taxidermy fish, from Second Home, and sea green walls.

I had questioned the wisdom of opening so far from the more prosperous end of town, but the recent influx of economic exiles from Brighton's astronomic prices had proved me wrong. Fusion cuisine based on Indian spices and fresh sea food had proved a hit with them. People who had saved tens of thousands buying a home had extra cash to spend. The wealthy clientele also liked to pop into my shop for a browse after lunch and I always placed something unique and expensive in the window display to encourage them. These clients adored upcycled and vintage furniture and never questioned my prices. After a morning of fobbing off rude questions, it always cheered me up to hear exclamations of delight as diners from Surfusion entered my doors.

Kieron, always a little snarky where I was concerned, had threatened to charge me a commission, but Rohan told him it worked both ways.

'Some people have started coming to lunch with us because they want to visit Tanya's shop,' he said. 'Maybe we should pay her?'

'We paid her enough for those taxidermy fish,' said Kieron. 'Daylight robbery.'

The Italian vases had been bought by an older couple on a post prandial wander from Surfusion. They had spotted the vases on my back shelf and couldn't disguise their glee. I knew I had a sale from the second they elbowed each other and gazed at the vases with longing. I even searched underneath the counter for a suitable piece of bubble wrap before they voiced their interest. They exited the shop beaming and promising to return, leaving me wondering where I'd stored the rest of my 60s Italian haul from the Bonetti's flat.

Mouse was due home from university at any minute, which increased my anticipation of arriving home. I couldn't wait to see him and hear all his news. To my surprise, it was not him, but Helen who waited for me at my house with an air of barely suppressed excitement. She always cooked George's dinner in the evenings and had it on the table for him promptly at seven o'clock. I looked at my watch. Ten to seven. I raised my eyebrows at her.

'Hi sis. What are you doing here? Won't George be expecting his food?'

She shook her head.

'He's gone to see DI Antrim in Brighton. They're going to have a pie and a pint and discuss some cold case they're working on. Anyway, I've got a surprise for you.'

'It's not Christmas yet. Shouldn't you keep your powder dry for now?'

'Too late. It's already happening. Shut your eyes.'

I sighed, but I did as I was told. Helen could get miffed if she sensed rebellion on my side. I would always be her little sister and fair game for being bossed around. She took my arm and led me through the sitting room to the back door. I heard it open and felt the rush of cold air against my shins.

'Okay. You can open them now.'

I did and had to blink several times to dispel the idea I was experiencing a mirage. My lovely back garden, with its banks of brambles and nettles had been savagely cut back, leaving a bare patch of earth with stalks protruding. The effect on me was the same as if Mouse had shaved off his black curls and turned into a skinhead. I gasped and shook my head. Helen squeaked with excitement.

'Doesn't it look wonderful? Of course, it's not finished yet, but when it is, you can plant a lawn and have some nice flowerbeds. The man told me it would take him another full day to finish.'

I opened my mouth, but nothing came out. Finally, I forced out a sentence.

'What have you done?'

Her smile faded.

'But you're always saying you're going to clean the back garden, and you never do, and I thought it would be a surprise and…'

She had been wounded by my reaction. Her voice caught in her throat. I tried to rearrange my features and say something positive.

'It's a lovely thought. I'm a little shocked at the difference that's all. I'll get used to it.'

'Get used to it? I thought you hated the brambles?'

'Well, yes, I did, sort of, but Hades loved them. And we got lots of blackberries.'

Her expression changed to one of fury. I flinched as I waited for her reply.

'Hades? You're worried about that mangy animal not liking the garden? He's not really yours, and he doesn't even like you.'

A low blow, and quite uncalled for. She could dish it out when she wanted.

'He does like me. He's just eccentric.'

'Eccentric? What's eccentric is your attachment to a cat who can't stand you. And being rude to me when I bought you a lovely present. I'll see myself out.'

She stomped to the front door and grabbed her coat from the stand. I let her go. I didn't feel like apologising. We could make up later when I got over the shock of my bald back garden. I shrugged and walked outside to inspect the damage. The almost bare earth radiated resentment at me as I kicked at it and tried to imagine a lawn where the jungle had been. I wondered where all the bickering sparrows had moved to. At least they didn't have any young or eggs. I tried to appreciate the eyesore being cleared, but I just felt depressed. Was I really the sort of person who had a lawn and flower beds with military lines of petunias?

Hades chose that exact moment to stalk out of the remaining patch of brambles. He sniffed the bare ground with barely concealed astonishment and looked around as if trying to recognise his surroundings. I called him, but he ignored me and entered the house, swishing his tail in anger. I followed him in, taking out a packet of his favourite food and squeezing into his dish. Predictably, he sniffed it and turned up his nose. Before I could complain, Harry came in through the front door, holding out a bulging paper bag.

'Who's hungry?' he said. 'I dropped by Mr Chen's and bought us a feast. Oh, and I found this young man outside begging for food.'

Mouse came in with his arms held open for a hug. I almost burst into tears of joy. The garden would keep.

Chapter 3

The next morning, Harry and I lingered over breakfast. He never liked me to fight with Helen. He had been estranged from his brother Nick for years before their reunion. They still had sticky patches because of their combustible relationship. I glance up from my toast.

'Should we invite Nick for lunch on Christmas day? I don't like to think of him alone in the cottage.'

'You just want to dilute George and Helen.'

I grinned.

'Maybe, but I would like him to come.'

'I'll think about it on my trip to London.'

'Okay, give my regards to Tommy. I don't suppose—'

'If you invite one cousin, you must invite them all. So, unless you are planning on building an extension in the back garden…'

'It's not even clear yet.'

After Harry had left, I searched under the kitchen sink until I found a pair of gardening gloves I'd bought in a fit of enthusiasm when I first moved into the Grotty Hovel. I had imagined clearing the back garden and turning it into a cute suburban garden with some bee magnets and wildflower patches. As time went by, I had become over fond of the bramble patch and Hades loved to roam in there pretending he was Tarzan so the gloves had not been used. They were cheap and made of flowery material. Who can resist a supermarket bargain buy of something you might need one day? I pulled them out and found that one of them had a large water stain and a patch of mould growing on it.

'But they're brand new,' I muttered to myself.

I cleared away the remains of breakfast and sat down to scroll through my messages with a second mug of tea. The front doorbell rang just as I was watching a man cutting logs without his shirt on, sent to me by Roz, I hasten to add. I opened the front door to someone remarkably similar looking and went beetroot red with unwarranted shame.

'Tanya?' he said. 'I'm Jeff, the gardener? I hope you were expecting me.'

I was paralysed for several seconds with images of stripper-grams running through my head before I recovered.

'Yes, of course. I'm sorry. I'm a little distracted this morning.'

'I'm not disturbing you; I hope.'

A wicked twinkle appeared in his eye.

'No, I, um. Why don't you go through to the garden? Do you want a cup of tea?'

'Not yet.'

'Watch out for the cat. He shouldn't go out on the street. He's not used to cars.'

'Do you mind if I wheel the rotavator through to the back garden? I'll try not to leave a trail of mud.'

'Not at all.'

The minute Jeff opened the front door again, Hades made a beeline for it. I was forced to bribe him into the kitchen with a second breakfast until Jeff had finished transferring his gear into the garden.

It didn't take him long to cut down the rest of the bramble thicket and the bed of nettles. Then he started up the rotavator with a couple of lusty pulls. I realised I had been staring mesmerised at his rather nice body and took myself back into the sitting room to fold laundry. Mouse slumped into a chair and held his head.

'What a racket! How's a man meant to sleep around here?'

'Maybe you could help the gardener? I'm sure he'd appreciate it.'

'If you make me a bacon sandwich while I get dressed.'

'Done.'

Soon Mouse had joined Jeff in the garden. They pulled up long root streamers from the soil and stuffed them into a large hessian bag with the other detritus. I watched from the backdoor with longing to join in. Mouse saw me lurking.

'Are you going to stand there all day? Come and help.'

I grabbed my gloves from the table and put them on. As I emerged, I noticed Jeff roll his eyes at Mouse. I went off him in a big way.

'What's wrong with my gloves?'

'Nothing. Get pulling,' said Mouse.

It's amazing how much quicker a job gets done with three people. We were soon left with just one stubborn root in the former nettle patch. All three of us got hold of it and pulled.

It felt like having a tug-of-war with the planet.

'It's coming,' said Jeff. 'Keep going.'

Suddenly, the earth released the root, and we all tumbled backwards onto the ground. A clod of material landed on my chest and I picked it up to examine it. I gasped and dropped it again, my heart hammering.

'You're not afraid of worms, are you?' said Jeff, trying to hide a sneer.

'Worms, no. Disembodied hands, yes.'

'Hands?' said Mouse. 'What hands? I—'

He poked at the clod with his toe and stopped mid-sentence.

'Is that a human hand?' said Jeff, who had gone pale.

'I think so,' I said.

'Definitely,' said Mouse.

I approached the hole left by the root and peered down. More bones were clearly visible poking out of the soil, gleaming white against the black earth.

I swallowed.

'I think someone may be buried here. We'd better call George.'

'And Flo.'

'Her too. George will be livid. How do we always end up with a body on our hands?'

Jeff's bravado had evaporated. He picked up his tools.

'I'd better be going,' he said, backing towards the door.

'Oh, you can't go now,' I said. 'You may have to give a statement.'

'A statement? I don't even know George. Why would I talk to him?'

'He's the local Detective Inspector,' said Mouse.

'I don't have to talk to the police. This is nothing to do with me.'

'It's nothing to do with us either,' I said.

Jeff's face revealed his doubts on that score, but he put his tools down again.

'I think I need that cup of coffee,' he said. 'Two sugars.'

I left Mouse in charge of the hot beverages and gave George a call. I cringed as he answered, dreading his reaction.

'Helen doesn't want to talk to you,' he said. 'How do you two always manage to upset each other? She only wanted to do something nice for you for Christmas.'

'I know. And I'm sorrier than you can imagine. Technically, the next thing I'm going to say is her fault.'

'I don't understand.'

'I'm afraid we found a body. Well, when I say we, I mean the gardener, the one Helen hired.'

'A body? Where?'

'Buried in the garden, here at the Grotty Hovel.'

'I wish you wouldn't call it that. It's a perfectly pleasant house. Is this a Christmas prank? Because I'm not in the mood.'

'I'm afraid not. The hand flew out of the ground and landed on my chest.'

I heard him snort in disbelief.

'Stay put. And don't let the gardener leave. I'll call in the forensic team and get Flo over too.'

It didn't take long for the forensic team to turn up. I knew most of them on sight by now. I sent Mouse to the local shop to buy supplies of milk and biscuits. George arrived, tutting and shaking his head at me.

'Another one,' he said. 'In the run up to Christmas too. Your timing is horrible.'

'Your girlfriend dug up my garden without my permission.'

'She's your sister.'

'You bought the house.'

'They didn't advertise it for sale with a semi-detached body in the back garden.'

I couldn't help laughing. He shrugged and grinned at me.

'Let's get on with it then.'

Chapter 4

It took most of the day for forensics to unearth the remaining bones and pack them carefully for transport. They painstakingly probed the soil for clues, picking up insects and pupae with tweezers and storing them in sample bags. They photographed the bones in situ before removing them for examination in Flo's pathology lab. The garden was roped off with yellow police tape for the time being, as the grave had not been filled again. Several of the technicians would come back to sift the soil through sieves before replacing it in the hole. If the clearance of the bramble jungle had left the garden desolate, the addition of an open grave had made it into a wasteland. I mourned its former state. The yellow police tape hanging loose from the back door proved irresistible to Hades who attacked it with vigour.

George and Flo stayed for a cup of tea after the others had left. Flo Barrington had been the local consulting forensic examiner for as long as I could remember. Her large physical presence, often swathed in elaborate outfits of brightly coloured silk, topped with a theatrical cloak, gave her an intimidating air, but she had the softest heart in town. Mouse adored her and they had their own private mutual admiration club. He plied her with biscuits and tea after she removed her coverall and hairnet. She gathered up all the stray hairs which had escaped from her bun, making it resemble a bird's nest. Her brow shone with effort as she sipped her tea.

'The body is definitely male, and from the look of his skull, he didn't die of old age,' she said.

'Someone murdered him?' said Mouse.

'I can't say that with certainty yet, but I think so.'

George sighed.

'I don't have the man power to investigate this properly before Christmas. Most of my team has taken time off to be with their families.'

'It might be hard to identify him too. He doesn't have any teeth left and the chances of his DNA being on the system are remote to say the least,' said Flo.

'How long has it been since his burial?' said Mouse.

'I can't be sure yet, but the insect life suggests less than five years.'

'But who buried him?' I asked. 'Isn't it illegal to plant someone in your garden?'

'Weirdly not,' said George. 'As long as you register the death with the Registrar, and get consent from the local authority for the burial, there's no law against it.'

'So, this might be a legal burial?' asked Mouse.

'It's possible, but we need a cause of death stated on the certificate to be sure.'

'And if there's no certificate registered?'

'It's an illegal burial, and I think somebody may have murdered him.'

'I'll ask Ghita to check with the council if you like,' I said. 'I think she still has access to the records department over there.'

George rolled his eyes.

'Okay, but no investigating without asking me.'

'Could it be a former occupant of the house?' I said. 'Maybe it was accidental?'

'I doubt his head was caved in accidentally,' said Flo, brushing crumbs off her blouse.

'Who did you buy the house from, Dad?' said Mouse.

'That sounds like an intent to investigate to me,' said George, frowning. 'I bought it from a man in a hurry to sell.'

'So, it was cheap?' I said. 'That explains the décor.'

George pursed his lips.

'He seemed like a bit of a spiv to me. He wanted a quick sale for cash.'

'Did he live here before selling the house?' said Mouse.

'I don't think so. He only had the property for a few months after buying it at auction. He put on a new roof and renovated the bathroom. Then he sold it to me.'

'Who did he buy it from?' I asked.

'I don't know,' said George.

'The internet does,' said Mouse.

'We need to identify the body before we do any investigating,' said George. 'Let Flo do her job first.'

'Of course,' I said.

As soon as George and Flo had left, Mouse opened his laptop and tapped away at the keys.

'What are you looking for?' I asked.

'I've already found it. The bloke who sold George the house was called Shawn Denny. He has an office above the chippy on the High Street.'

'Can you call him and make an appointment for tomorrow morning? I think I'll pop to the shop for a while and see how Ghita managed without me. I'll be back for supper. Do you want a takeaway?'

'Isn't Harry bringing lamb chops from his cousin's butcher shop?'

'I had completely forgotten. See you later then. Happy hunting.'

Ghita Chowdhury was the third of the three musketeers in my friendship group, which included her, myself and Roz Murray. She spent a lot of time at the Surfusion restaurant with Rohan and Kieron, but often helped me at Second Home. Ghita was petite and shy, with long dark hair in a plait which hung almost to her bottom and a habit of standing on tiptoe to make herself more visible. She cooked like a goddess and supplied amazing cakes to me for the Vintage Café on the upper floor of Second Home. She also magicked up astounding new recipes for Surfusion, which transported you to Nirvana when the food reached your taste buds. She helped me in the shop too, fending off the rudest of questions with shy smiles and an obdurate attitude. Her face lit up as I entered, but before she could say anything, Roz bounded down the stairs from the café, eyes glistening with malice. News travelled fast in Seacastle.

'Is it true? The town is abuzz with speculation.'

I rolled my eyes at her.

'Trust you to find out.'

'Her phone hasn't stopped pinging all afternoon,' said Ghita. 'I've got a headache.'

'My contacts are desperate for gossip,' said Roz. 'You are like a body magnet. How do you do it? If you had the same effect on fish, Ed would tie you to the mast.'

I sighed and wished he had tied Roz to the mast instead.

'I can't tell you any details yet.'

'But you can tell us something, right?'

'The gardener dug up a human hand. Well, the bones of one.'

'The gardener? Since when can you afford a gardener?' said Ghita. 'You don't even pay us most of the time.'

'Helen hired him to clear the back garden. Without telling me, I might add.'

'Is he cute?' said Roz.

'He looks like the lumberjack video you sent me. But unfortunately, the insides do not match the pretty packaging.'

'I don't care. I'm as shallow as a puddle.'

'We know,' said Ghita. 'Tell us about the body, Tan.'

'After we found the hand, the forensic team turned up at the Grotty Hovel and dug up a complete skeleton. Flo thinks he was murdered.'

'It's a man? That's novel. Isn't it unwanted wives that get buried in back gardens?' said Roz.

'We don't know he was murdered yet. It might be a legal garden burial.'

'Ooh. How creepy. I can't believe you've been living with a body all that time,' said Ghita.

'It's no worse than living with George all that time,' I said.

Roz guffawed.

'I can't believe you said that.'

'Neither can I. Let's have a cup of tea and count the till receipts.'

'That won't take long,' said Ghita.

'Happy Christmas to you too.'

Chapter 5

Shawn Denny, the former owner of the Grotty Hovel, ran a business flipping properties after doing the bare minimum to upgrade them to a habitable state. The High Street building which housed his office had seen better days. The shopfront paint had mostly peeled off, and I noticed cracks between the window frame and the brickwork. I pressed the doorbell with caution and the door clicked open.

'Come on up,' said a voice. 'I'm on the second floor.'

I climbed up the steep stairs, wishing I had brought reinforcements, but Mouse had stayed in the Vintage to deal with the lunchtime rush and Harry was helping Max Wong, our friendly, upmarket competition, with a van delivery. The carpet on stairs felt sticky underfoot and the stairway stank of rancid fat, making me wrinkle my nose in disgust. I wondered when it had last been cleaned. Shawn Denny sat behind a metal desk in a cheap, shiny suit. His top shirt buttons were open, showing a scrawny chest with sparse hairs. A fan heater blew a stream of hot air straight at me, making me feel sick.

'Buying or selling?' he said, with his finger hovering over a grubby tablet.

'Neither. I'm hoping you can give me some information about one property which passed through your books.'

His eyes narrowed.

'What's your name?'

'Tanya Bowe.'

'No, it's not. It's Tanya Carter, isn't it? I knew I recognised you. You used to be married to the local DI.'

'It's Tanya Bowe now. I'm divorced.'

'Oh, I already know that. He bought a house from me for the settlement. I'm not getting involved in any disputes about property values. Your divorce is not my business. You can leave now.'

He stood up, but I remained sitting down.

'I don't care what my house cost. I can look it up on Right Move if I really want to find out. The police found a body in the back garden and—'

He backed into the wall, pale as snow.

'They found what? You're not pinning that on me. I've got rights.'

I raised an eyebrow and sighed loudly.

'I'm not trying to. The body was buried years ago, before I moved in, and before you did the house up.'

'So why are you here?'

'I need to know who you bought the property from.'

His shoulders slumped.

'That's all?'

'That's all. I swear.'

He shrugged and pulled out a drawer in his desk, shuffling through some scruffy papers.

'Jay and Lorna Nuttall. They live in Shoreham now.'

He scribbled their address on a scrap of paper.

'Here. Take it and go. I don't want to see you again.'

'Thanks. The feeling's mutual.'

I stuffed the piece of paper into my handbag and left the office without touching anything. Shawn Denny had not endeared himself to me, but I could see his point of view. Who would want to be linked to a murder? I walked down the high street, stopping to admire Grace and Max Wong's Asian Antique Emporium. Grace had outdone herself with the window dressing. Red silk bedcovers were artistically draped over a series of different levels and covered in small parcels covered in multicoloured, metallic paper with red velvet ribbons. As I gazed in wonder at the display, it reminded me I still hadn't hung as much as a bauble in the shop or at home. Two large boxes of tinsel and baubles sat unused at the back of Second Home, waiting for me to bring the Christmas spirit to the shop.

I popped into the bakery and bought some chocolate croissants, still warm from the oven. I intended to use them as bribes for Mouse, Ghita and Roz, to get them to put up the decorations. The temptation to tuck into the delicious pastries made me walk faster, and I arrived panting at the door.

'Why are you out of breath?' said Mouse. 'Did he chase you?'

'Croissant longing.'

'That's a thing?'

'It is now. I—'

Then Mouse lifted my chin up.

'Look,' he said.

I did and gasped. The interior of the shop had been transformed. Tinsel had been strung amongst the glass floats on the ceiling, giving it the air of a festive disco. Swedish wicker reindeer and strings of winged angels decorated the furniture. Baubles twinkled from every corner. I had forgotten all about finding the Swedish decorations in a clearance months before. The effect wasn't as glamorous as Grace's décor, but it looked bright and cosy. Roz, Ghita and Mouse had brought Christmas to Second Home, and it made me feel quite overwhelmed.

'It's wonderful,' I said. 'Definitely worth a croissant.'

'They smell fabulous. Are they still warm?' said Roz. I nodded.

'Let's have a coffee upstairs and celebrate the decorations.'

We went upstairs and sat where we could hear anyone entering the shop. Not that we had many shoplifters. Thieves did not appreciate second-hand junk and could not sell it on anyway. The cash register did not exactly bulge either.

We were soon seated at the window table with croissant crumbs down our fronts and milky coffee moustaches like children at a milk break. I handed round some paper napkins.

'What did Shawn Denny say about the Grotty Hovel?' said Mouse, wiping his lip.

'The estate agent?' said Roz. 'Why did you go and see him? Don't tell me you're investigating the body in the garden? Can't you give it a rest for Christmas?'

I frowned.

'How can I? Someone murdered that poor man and buried him in a shallow grave. He won't have any more Christmases. I owe it to him to find out what happened, so he can rest in peace.'

'What about his family?' said Ghita. 'Why haven't they reported him missing?'

'Maybe he didn't have one. Flo said he had no teeth, so he may have been old when he died.'

'Maybe they got rid of him for their inheritance?' said Mouse. 'Now that the police have dug him up, there's room to bury someone else.'

He squeaked as I aimed a punch at his arm.

'Hilarious.'

'Did Shawn have any useful information?' said Roz.

'He gave me the names of the couple who sold him the house. I thought we could ask them about its history.'

'Why would they tell you anything?' said Ghita.

'I'm a journalist, remember? I'll say I'm doing research for a story. Most people love to talk about themselves, even more so when they are interviewed by a famous T.V. personality.'

Roz raised her eyebrows.

'I'm not sure a researcher on a crime show counts in that category, but they won't know the difference.'

'Thanks for your vote of confidence. Oh, by the way, thank you all for decorating the shop. It looks wonderful.'

'Ghita did most of it. She's the arty one,' said Mouse. 'I'm just tall and can put tinsel up in hard-to-reach places.'

'Everywhere's hard to reach if you're Ghita,' said Roz, sniggering.

'That's way harsh,' said Mouse.

Ghita pouted.

'It's not my fault I'm short. You're so mean.'

'Ghita may be petite, but she has an enormous character,' I said. 'And she can still wear children's clothes. She's very economical to run.'

'I won't make any more cakes for the Vintage if you're rude to me.'

'We're only joking. You look lovely in your school uniform,' said Roz.

'Honestly, Roz. Leave Ghita alone. The joke will be on you one of these days.'

I put my arm around Ghita's shoulder.

'Can you make something delicious for Christmas week? Maybe a dash of cherry brandy in the mix?'

Her face lit up.

'Of course. Will I make two in case you want to take one home?'

'Make three and I'll take one too,' said Roz.

'Only if you stop the short jokes.'

'Scout's honour.'

'You were a girl guide,' I said.

'More coffee?' said Mouse.

Chapter 6

We drove to Shoreham under a pitch-black overcast sky to see the Nuttalls the next evening. They lived on a new housing estate just to the north of the estuary. The neat, detached houses followed a winding driveway which doubled back on itself before looping around to join the original entrance. Their house sat at the back of the estate, and as we neared it, Harry chortled.

'There's nothing like a bit of Christmas spirit,' he said.

I stared in awe at their house, which was lit up like a Christmas tree. It had been outlined with multicoloured bulbs. Several large light sculptures stood resplendent in the garden; one of a sleigh and reindeer picked out in red and green bulbs and the other an angel in white. A neon banner over the front door flashed on and off, wishing us a Merry Christmas. The overall effect was uber festive.

'Oh my goodness. I thought the Oxford Street decorations were over the top.'

'Blimey! Can you imagine the size of their electricity bill?' said Harry.

'And the massive amount of work to put all those lights up? That's dedication for you.'

'They must be massive fans of Christmas.'

When Lorna Nuttall came to the front door dressed as an elf, I had to pretend to have a coughing fit to hide the fact I had guffawed in amazement. She was tall and thin with a beaky nose, and not at all elf-like. Harry slapped me hard on the back, leaving me breathless.

'I'm sorry,' he said. 'She's allergic.'

My eyes watered with effort as I tried not to laugh. Lorna seemed oblivious to the effect her outfit had had on us. She brought us into her sitting room where Jay Nuttall, also dressed as an elf, sat on an armchair covered in a sequined blanket depicting Rudolf, standing at a bar. He had a pair of pixie boots with bells on the pointy toes. The entire room twinkled and flashed and blinded us with a multitude of lights and shiny decorations. Harry leaned over to mutter in my ear.

'I should've brought my shades.'

Lorna left the room again.

'She's gone to get the eggnog,' said Jay. 'She'll be back shortly. We like the Aldi one best.'

I felt as if I had gone to sleep and woken up in Santa's grotto. I looked around the extraordinary sitting room. They must have expended a massive amount of energy to create it.

'You like Christmas then?' said Harry.

I had to look at the floor to avoid catching his eye. Lorna saved me by bustling in with a tray containing glasses of eggnog and some mince pies.

'I love dressing up. I've got lots of outfits. It's our favourite time of the year, isn't it, honey?'

Jay nodded, without enthusiasm I thought. Perhaps he joined in for love.

'Yes, cupcake.'

'You haven't changed much,' said Lorna, looking at me. 'I remember you from Uncovering the Truth. I wish they'd do another series. It was one of our favourite programmes.'

'Thank you,' I said. 'I don't think we're as young as we used to be. The hours were horrendous.'

'What did you want to ask us about if it's not for the programme?' said Jay.

'I believe you used to own a terraced house on Keat's Road in Seacastle?'

'Not me. My mother, Daphne. She lived there for about forty years; I think. I was born and brought up there.'

'Did your father live there too?'

Lorna bit her lip. Jay frowned.

'That bastard never lived with her. He was one and done.'

'Don't say that. We don't know what happened to him.'

'Did he disappear?' said Harry.

'He joined the army, and he never came back. He had no idea my mother got pregnant.'

'I'm ex-army. Which regiment did he join?'

'I don't know,' said Lorna. 'My mother didn't tell me.'

'What was his name?' I asked.

'Why are you asking me about him? He's been gone for forty years.'

'He never came back?'

'Not as far as I know. My mother wouldn't have told me anyway. Can you please tell me why you are asking me?'

'I'm really sorry, but the police have found a man's body in the garden. I wondered if you might know who it is?'

'Are you accusing my mother of murder?'

'They're saying she murdered your father,' said Jay, bristling with fury.

'No, that's not it at all,' I said. 'I'm sorry I gave you that impression. We're trying to find out if anyone was buried in the garden while your mother lived at the property.'

'She means legally,' said Harry. 'It's personal for us. We live there now.'

'You live there? Why didn't you say so?'

'I apologise for jumping the gun,' I said. 'I'm so determined to find out what happened that I walked all over your feelings. We can leave if you are upset.'

Jay exchanged looks with Lorna.

'No. That's okay. We got off on the wrong foot, but nothing another eggnog won't cure. How can we help you?'

'I'm not sure the police will be able to identify the body because of the lack of evidence. The skull had no teeth and I doubt there is DNA on file for him.'

'So, they can't identify him?'

'It's not looking good. Did your mother have a partner?' I asked Lorna.

'Oh. No. She never met anyone else. She lived alone there until she died three years ago.'

'Did you move in to the house after she died?'

'No, I couldn't face it. We love our new house and the people on our estate. The house sat empty before Mr Denny offered to buy it from us. To tell the truth, I couldn't wait to get rid of it.'

'Maybe someone took advantage of the vacant property to stash a body in the garden?' said Jay.

'That's a possibility. I guess I'll have to wait for the police to do the autopsy.'

Lorna squinted at me.

'But why are you so interested?'

'Because nobody else is. I can't bear the thought of him going missing and nobody caring enough to look for him.'

'And she never comes across a mystery she doesn't want to solve,' said Harry.

'I'll refill the eggnog,' said Lorna. 'Would you like to see photographs of the house from years ago?'

'I'd love that,' I said.

'These mince pies are fantastic,' said Harry. 'I'm going to need another one.'

Lorna grinned.

'My mother's recipe. She'd have loved you. She always did like a soldier.'

Chapter 7

Following what turned out to be an interesting evening at the Nuttall's house, my investigation into the identity of the body in the garden threatened to grind to a halt. I had no leads left after the only one turned out to be a dead end. It gave me a timeframe for the burial of the body, but no clue as to its origin. I tried not to obsess about the mystery, but I found it difficult. I put all my effort into selling vintage goods at Second Home and wearing a veneer of Christmas cheer.

The news I had been waiting for finally came from Flo, who took pity on me and dropped in for a browse and a coffee. She selected two silk lampshades in a gorgeous plum colour and a cute mini-ottoman footstool covered in Persian carpet. I suspected she bought them for herself, but I did not ask her. She came upstairs for a coffee and a piece of Ghita's tipsy cherry Christmas cake, which had proved a roaring success. Ghita had made several replacement cakes with no sign of a dip in demand. I could tell Flo had news, from the way she kept fiddling with the buttons on her blouse. She would never win at poker, her tells were obvious to anyone.

'This cake should be illegal,' she said, hoovering up the crumbs with her finger tip and sucking them off. 'Ghita must have picked up some black magic from the local coven.'

'She wouldn't come into a room if she thought there was a witch present. She's got a permanent veto on any form of sorcery.'

'Can you cut me a second slice for taking home? I may not be able to sleep thinking about this cake. I need emergency rations.'

I smiled and picked out a large piece for her, which I wrapped in a couple of napkins. She put it carefully into her large leather handbag. I refilled her cup and waited.

'I got the results of the autopsy,' she said finally.

'Which one? Oh, you mean the body in my garden?' I said, feigning innocence.

Flo snorted.

'As if you didn't know. You look as if you're about to burst with impatience.'

'Well, stop being mean then, and tell me all about it.'

'His name was Cyril Prout. We identified him from the registration number on his hip implant. The poor man was eighty-two years old, but he didn't die of old age. Somebody murdered him and buried him in your garden.'

'Why did they choose the Grotty Hovel?'

'He used to live next door. The house they turned into an Airbnb. Where you found Hades? That house belonged to him.'

I couldn't have been more astonished.

'He owned the house next door? How strange. Maybe he owned Hades too?'

'That's a possibility. Have you ever had his chip checked by the vet?'

'We don't even know if he has one.'

'You've never taken Hades to the vet?'

'Have you seen how he treats me? If I tried to put him in a carry box, I'd end up going to accident and emergency myself.'

'Couldn't Mouse do it?'

I frowned.

'I don't think we really want to know who owns Hades, in case we have to give him back.'

'Don't you have any way of identifying him?'

'There's an old collar he was wearing when I found him, but Mouse took it off. I don't know if he kept it.'

'Maybe you should ask him.'

'Perhaps. What will happen to Prout's body?'

'We have organised a burial service for him on Wednesday afternoon at two o'clock. I wondered if you might like to come with Mouse, Harry and Helen to swell the numbers? It seems so sad to bury him with no mourners.'

'Of course we'll come.'

I wondered if the Nuttalls had known Cyril. Perhaps they would come if I let them know about his passing.

'That would be great. I'm sure he'd appreciate it.'

'Does he have any family?'

'Not that we know of, but maybe Mouse could perform some magic and dig up a cousin of some sort?'

'I'll ask him. What are you doing on Christmas day, Flo?'

'The usual, I suppose. Eating and reading and watching repeats on the television.'

'That sounds wonderful. I've got Helen and George coming over to the Grotty Hovel for Christmas lunch. I'm dreading it.'

'Christmas is the season of goodwill.'

'I'll try to remember that.'

After Flo had left, I rang Lorna Nuttall.

'Hello, it's Tanya Bowe here.'

'Tanya? What a surprise! Is there something you forgot to ask us?'

'No. Well, I might have some more questions now because something's come up.'

'Have they identified the body? I thought it was impossible.'

'They found a serial number on his hip implant. They say his name was—'

'Cyril? Oh my goodness. I knew it. I told Jay after you and Harry had left. We didn't want to jump the gun, though.'

'You knew Mr Prout?'

'Of course. He was my mother Daphne's dear friend and neighbour for many years.'

'I'm so sorry. I had no idea.'

'Oh, I didn't know him well, but until she died, she and Cyril were very close.'

'They used to pop into each other's houses all the time. But they had a tiff not long before she passed.'

'A tiff? Do you know what about?'

'I know this sounds silly, but she was jealous of his girlfriend.'

'His girlfriend?'

'Yes, he met her at the Veterans' Club. My mother called her a blonde hussy, but I'm sure she was just jealous. Daphne had been alone for so many years. She had a crush on Cyril, but I don't think it was mutual.'

'I see.'

But I didn't. I wondered if it was her motive, no matter how farfetched. Would a lonely pensioner murder another if he fancied someone else?

'Was there something else you wanted?'

'Oh, I nearly forgot. Mr Prout's funeral is at Saint Laurence's church on Wednesday at two o'clock. Would you like to come? We're trying to find people who knew him so he doesn't get buried alone.'

'I'd love to be there for him. My mother would be pleased. And I can visit her grave while I'm there.'

Chapter 8

Saint Laurence's Church sat on the outskirts of Seacastle, surrounded by a dark ribbon of poplar trees. Its impressive size and lofty spire were echoes of a time when the population flocked to Sunday worship instead of shopping centres. Behind it, an expansive graveyard had been laid out in neat rows, but older tombs huddled together close to the walls of the church, a jumble of lids and headstones with upturned inscriptions obliterated by moss and weather. The cavernous interior emphasised the sparse attendance, but contrary to my expectations, we were not the only souls who had assembled to see Cyril Prout off the mortal coil.

Besides me, Mouse and Harry, George and Helen had turned up with Flo and DS Joe Brennan from the station. A plump, harassed looking woman in a tight navy suit gave me a smile from her bench in front of ours, which she occupied with several ancient ladies in dowager outfits, competing to appear the most devastated. I recognised one lady from my street and gave her a tentative wave. I hadn't got to know any of my neighbours despite living in the Grotty Hovel for nearly two years. Modern life kept everyone too busy to stand on their doorsteps and gossip in the street. Instead, people watched actors pretending to gossip on their television streets shut off from their neighbours.

The vicar whizzed us through the service without ceremony and gave a short eulogy lacking in any detail, which made me sad. We were soon standing beside the open grave, in a cool breeze which whipped through the poplars, watching Cyril's coffin being lowered inside. The coffin appeared simple but sturdy with a small brass plaque on the lid. I could make out Cyril's name and the date of birth, but no date of death. I wondered who had paid for the funeral. A tear ran down my cheek, surprising me with its stealth. I made a silent promise to Cyril I'd find his killer and wished him a sound sleep as the earth thudded on his coffin.

'I didn't know Cyril had relatives,' said a voice.

I turned around to find the woman in the navy suit standing behind me. There was something about her I thought I recognised, but the funeral had disconnected my brain. I couldn't think where I might have seen her before.

'Oh, we're not relatives. The police found Cyril in our back garden.'

She blushed to the roots of her hair.

'How stupid of me. I should have known. I apologise. My name's Violet Kent. I'm the manager at the centre.'

'The centre?'

'The Veterans' Club. Cyril used to be a regular visitor.'

'Did Cyril have any living family members?'

'None that I know of, not that he was alone,' she said, tapping the side of her nose.

'Are you referring to his girlfriend?'

She laughed.

'You mean girlfriends? Cyril played the field.'

She glanced at the old ladies who were leaving the cemetery arm in arm, hobbling on arthritic legs and jerked her head towards them. I would have liked to speak to our neighbour, but she and her friend were embroiled in a hissed conversation which didn't invite interruption. I decided to knock on her door after I got home.

'His fan club,' said Violet, looking at her watch. 'The rumour mill will go into overdrive now. They just can't help themselves. They've got a bee in their bonnet about Daphne Sands too. One of them told me Lorna might have killed Daphne, but everybody knows she fell down the stairs. Anyway, Lorna loved her mother. You don't want to pay them any mind. They watch too many crime thrillers on the telly.'

'Would you like to have a coffee with us? We'd love to know more about him.'

'I'm sorry, but I have to be back at the centre for tea time or the regulars will die of thirst. You can come by any time for a chat, though.'

'I'd like that if I can fit it in. I own a shop which sells vintage goods on the High Street and the Christmas rush is starting. Let me see what I can do.'

Violet nodded and rushed off after the two ladies. I looked around for Lorna Nuttall and spotted her heading away from the grave. I trotted to catch up with her, my boots crunching on the gravel. She spun around with an unwelcoming expression on her face, but I pretended I hadn't seen it.

'Can I come with you?' I asked. 'I'd like to ask you some more questions about Cyril.'

'I'm going to see my mother,' she said. 'I like to go on my own.'

I got the hint and wandered back to where Harry and Mouse were chatting with Helen and George. Then I saw someone I recognised, sitting on a bench outside the church. She had golden hair piled in a bun under a small black fascinator. Gladys Fitch pulled her coat tightly around her as I approached. From her puffy cheeks, I suspected she had been crying. Could she be involved in this mystery too? Recognition dawned on her face when I smiled at her.

'Tanya! What are you doing here?'

'I could ask you the same question.'

'It seems we need a chat. Is your offer of a coffee at Second Home still open?'

'Of course. Can we give you a lift?'

'Are you going to introduce us?' said George, leaning over my shoulder.

'If you like. Gladys Fitch, this is my ex-husband DI George Carter and my sister, Helen Bowe.'

'Charmed, I'm sure,' said Gladys.

'Aren't you the lady who helped us with the Surfusion inquiry?' said Joe Brennan. 'We couldn't have solved it without your photograph.'

'That's me,' said Gladys, going pink with pleasure.

'What are you doing here today? Don't tell me you knew Cyril too?' said George.

'We're about to find out,' I said, wishing I could elbow him.

'Can we come too?' said Helen. 'It's so intriguing to have a body in Tanya's garden.'

I rolled my eyes.

'Okay. Let's all meet at the Vintage. Come on Gladys. My car's in the car park.'

I glanced backwards and saw Lorna Nuttall in the distance. I considered inviting her, but I didn't know if she would recognise Gladys and I had a sneaking suspicion Gladys might be the blonde hussy so despised by her mother. I texted ahead to Roz, to warn her of the coming invasion of the Vintage and asked her to arrange the chairs and tables into one long seating area. She sent me a row of open-mouthed emojis and asked me to pick up some milk on my way there. I dropped Mouse at the

Co-Op and Gladys at the door of Second Home and went to park in a side street.

By the time I got back to the shop, everybody had settled themselves upstairs, and I felt a frisson of excitement course through my veins. Roz and Mouse had already started a production line of coffee and cake as I got to the top of the stairs to the Vintage. Gladys had parked her large black handbag beside her and she picked it up as I arrived, indicating I should sit in its place. I noticed that Flo and Joe Brennan had been banished back to the station and only George remained in an official capacity.

'Will you start first?' said Gladys. 'I need to know what you know before I explain.'

'We found a body in Tanya's back garden,' said George. 'It was identified as Cyril Prout. Forensics showed he had been murdered.'

'We know he used to live next door to us, but when we moved in two years ago, our house had been vacant for a while,' I said.

'This means the police have no idea how Cyril's body got there, or even an approximate date for his murder. The entomologists are studying the fauna from the site and will report back to us soon. Any information you can give me which might help with the background to his death, and the timeline of events, would be of a great help to the investigation. We are short staffed because of the proximity of Christmas, hence this impromptu interview. I may need you to make a statement down at the station if you prove to have important information on the case.'

I tried not to show my irritation at George's pomposity. Gladys didn't seem to notice. She sipped her tea and pursed her lips. Then, she shut her eyes as if attempting to pin down a memory. She opened them again and nodded briskly.

'Right. Well then. Cyril's death has come out of the blue. It has been a terrible shock to me, or should I say the manner of it? Cyril and I were an item. We met at the Veterans' Club on an open day. I served in a confidential unit during the Cold War and he had been overseas to Eastern Europe many times with his regiment, so we had a lot in common. We hit it off from our first meeting and were rarely apart after that. I practically lived at the house on Keat's Road for a while. We had a passionate relationship there. I can't believe you live next door now. What an extraordinary coincidence!'

'I don't think so. Tanya's always finding bodies,' muttered George.

'That isn't what she meant,' I said, glaring at him. 'What broke up your relationship?'

'We never broke up. Well, not exactly.'

She swallowed and took another sip of her tea. Silence reigned in the shop as she gathered herself again. She wiped her lip with a linen handkerchief embroidered with tiny blue flowers.

'I received a text message from Cyril telling me he had left for Turkey on an archaeological trip. I found it shocking he hadn't talked to me before leaving, as he would have known how much I would have wanted to join him on the trip. But he didn't answer my messages about it. Radio silence, you know. And he never returned. Finally, he sent me a text saying he had met somebody on the trip and that he wouldn't be coming home. I wondered if he had been two-timing me with someone else from the Club. Every woman there wanted to get their claws into him. He had that way about him.'

'Is there anyone who might have been jealous about him getting together with you?' said George.

She laughed.

'All of them.'

George cleared his throat.

41

'Anyone in particular?'

'His neighbour, Daphne, who lived in your house, Tanya. She had an embarrassing crush on Cyril. She was always hanging around, cooking him hotpots and cakes and suchlike. At first, I thought she might have run off with him, when I didn't see her again either. But she's buried at Saint Laurence's too, so she can't have gone with him.'

'How long has she been dead?' I asked.

'I'm not sure. Cyril disappeared during my stay in the hospital. He was incommunicado for a while and then I got those messages about his trip. My recovery was slow, and it took me a long time to recover enough to venture out of my flat. I heard about Daphne's death much later. I haven't been back to the club since.'

'Can you give me any helpful dates? I'd love to get a timeline on Cyril's disappearance,' said George.

'I can't remember offhand, but it was about three years ago. We always signed a register at the Veterans' Club when we popped in. The last time I saw Cyril, we went to a showing of "A Matter of Life and Death" there. They used to have movie nights once a month. What a lovely film that is. It starred David Niven, my favourite.'

'We're going to need a statement,' said George. 'There's no need for you to come to the station now that I think about it. How about if I send DS Brennan around to your flat?'

'That would be fine. He can text me a time for us to meet up,' said Gladys. She staggered to her feet. 'I'm tired. I'd like to go home now.'

Harry who had been listening with rapt attention, stood up immediately and offered her his arm.

'Allow me to escort you,' he said, winking at me.

'It's only a block,' said Gladys. 'I'll be all right.'

'As an ex-member of the armed forces, I can't let you do that, I'm afraid. I insist on giving you a guard of honour.'

She bit her lip in pleasure and allowed him to help her on with her coat. They disappeared down the stairs, and I heard the doorbell clang. George sighed.

'You know how much I hate you interfering with police business,' he said. 'But this is a delicate case so close to Christmas. The suspects are all octogenarians and may not be with us much longer. Could you please see the manager of the Veterans' Club and try to winkle the dates of Cyril's last visit from her? I'd also like any gossip you can gather about the ladies in his life. Our boy seems to have been quite a character.'

I grinned.

'I thought you'd never ask.'

Chapter 9

After George and Helen left, Roz, Mouse, Harry and I sat discussing the ramifications of Gladys's relationship with Cyril. Many of us are guilty of ageism without being conscious of it, and I felt uncomfortable with some of my earlier assumptions. I had noticed George wincing when Gladys implied that her relationship with Cyril had been physical. As usual, Roz was in her element. She loved gossip more than anything, except Ed, and the idea of a murder committed by a jealous widow or spinster was like catnip for her.

'This is surreal,' she said. 'If someone had told me a bunch of octogenarians would be the prime suspects for a brutal murder, I would have laughed in their face.'

'They may be old, but their essence remains the same despite the passage of time,' said Harry. 'The fact they are ex-service personnel adds the possibility that some of them may have killed before.'

He winked at me. I must have appeared startled as I realised the implication. He rolled his eyes at my consternation.

'I don't think we can make any assumptions about them,' I said.

'And you didn't?' said Roz.

'Of course I did, but this investigation is making me examine my prejudices. We'll all be old soon.'

'Speak for yourself,' said Mouse.

'Gladys Fitch is an independent and courageous woman. I doubt she has changed much since her days in the service. She's certainly not as frail as she appears. I don't like to point this out, but she had spent a lot of time at Keat's Road, and she would have had access to our garden through the fence,' said Harry.

'Are you saying she could be a suspect in Cyril's murder?' said Mouse.

Harry shrugged. 'Yup.'

'He's right though,' I said. 'There's nothing left to back up her story about Cyril's phantom trip to Turkey. The text messages she claimed to have received from Cyril would be long gone by now.'

'You might get some corroboration from the Veterans' Club,' said Roz. 'I couldn't believe it when George asked you to help.'

'There's a first time for everything,' said Mouse. 'Maybe it's the Christmas spirit.'

'Never look a gift horse in the mouth. Even if it's an early Christmas present,' said Harry.

'That's what landed us in trouble in the first place,' I said.

'What do you mean?' said Roz.

'Helen paid for the gardener to clear the jungle at the back of our house. That's when we found the body.'

'I bet George wishes you'd found it after Christmas. Now he had to ask you for help. He must have hated that.'

'Poor George. I bet he gets ribbed down at the station about Tanya. Imagine having an ex-wife who's a body magnet,' said Harry.

'Jessica Fletcher is my spirit animal.'

'I thought that was a mouse,' said Harry, causing me to grin at my stepson.

'Well, it's definitely not my grumpy rescue cat.'

'Is he still ignoring you?' said Roz. 'He's so stubborn.'

'I've given up, really. I might get a proper cat.'

'Don't be mean. Hades is traumatised. He thinks you trapped him in that basket.'

'Traumatised? What about me? I go through a packet of Band Aids monthly, patching up the scratches.'

'Never mind Hades,' said Harry. 'Have you considered the role that the Veterans' Club plays in this story?'

'What do you mean?' said Roz.

'In my experience, veterans' clubs have mostly male members because in those days, women were not accepted in the ranks. They mostly did secretarial jobs and in the past were made to feel uncomfortable if they tried to join. Obviously, Gladys and her friends were exceptions. But the women who used to frequent the club were not the only ones who might have been jealous of Cyril and Gladys's relationship. What if other men at the club resented his popularity with the sparse female membership?' said Harry.

'I hadn't thought of that,' I said. 'You make a good point.'

'We'll make a detective of you yet,' said Mouse.

'I'm just using logic,' said Harry, but he beamed.

Sometimes Harry got left out when I investigated an unexplained death, but his logical thinking skills were second to none. He was also an excellent kisser. I refrained from reminding myself of those skills in front of Roz and Mouse, but I banked one to give him later.

'Right, I'm off to eat supper with Ed. He's making macaroni cheese tonight so I don't want to be late,' said Roz.

We washed up the cups and replaced the chairs and tables in their customary spots before locking up the shop. The normally dark street had been illuminated by the Christmas windows of the shops. The main window of Surfusion had been decorated with tinsel streamers resembling the edges of waves with shiny fish cut out of aluminium and coloured metallic wrapping paper. I suspected Ghita's involvement in this stunning creation. She really could do anything she turned her hand to. No wonder Rohan and Kieron treated her like a queen. They almost lost her through their petty jealousy and constant squabbling, but after her courageous exploits in their darkest hour, everything had been resolved. Or at least as resolved as a relationship between a gay couple and a single woman with a crush on both of them can be. I avoided the subject with her.

We drove home in the Mini, stopping on the way for a selection of curries and trimmings. We all munched poppadoms, covering the car in crumbs.

'Remind me to hoover out the car,' I said. 'Or we'll have a colony of mice making their home in here.'

'We could shut Hades in the car for an hour,' said Mouse

'Or a couple of days,' I said.

'He's not that bad,' said Harry.

'You don't have to pay for his cat food,' I said.

'The Christmas spirit is lacking in this droid,' said Mouse.

'Perhaps I should take her to buy a Christmas tree tomorrow?' said Harry.

'Already?' I said.

'Are you waiting until the last minute? They'll all be sold,' said Mouse. 'I'm dying to decorate the Grotty Hovel.'

I sighed.

'Let's go to the garden centre up by the Cissbury Ring tomorrow and see what they've got.'

'Excellent,' said Harry. 'We can take the van.'

Chapter 10

The next morning, Harry and I had a bacon sandwich before setting out for the Cissbury Ring. We took the sandwiches and a flask of tea to the local wind shelter where we stared out at the sea, each with our own thoughts. The wind shelter was my refuge and inspiration, especially when I struggled with life. On this morning, I tried to shake off my Grinch-like attitude to Christmas, a legacy of my marriage to George. This Christmas would be so much better. I had to admit that having Helen cooking most of the trimmings would lighten my burden. And having Harry living at the Grotty Hovel full time had made life fun again.

'I spoke to Nick,' said Harry.

'About Christmas? What did he say?'

Harry sighed.

'He refused to come. I don't know why. I'm pretty disappointed.'

My heart wept for him. Harry almost never admitted to any feelings other than those he had for me. He even struggled to show affection for Mouse, though I knew he would die for him if he had to.

'That's a blow. I'm so sorry, darling.'

'Why does he have to make everything so difficult? I thought we'd sorted things out, but he's still holding back on me.'

'Maybe he doesn't trust his own reaction. He could be afraid of the emotions he's suppressing.'

'I guess so. I don't like to think of him all alone in that mouldy cottage.'

'I thought you two had done it up.'

'Not completely. It's not really habitable, truth be told. He should bulldoze the house and start again.'

'Can he afford to do that?'

'Not really.'

A large seagull skittered to a halt in front of us and tilted his head to one side.

'Herbert? Is that you?' I said.

'I think so. He's got that slightly elongated red spot on his beak.'

'I can't believe he's back. I've missed him terribly.'

'Have you got any crusts left?'

'Yes, but I was going to give them to you.'

'I'll sacrifice just this once.'

I held out a crust to Herbert, but he did not approach me, so I threw it a few feet away from us. Herbert waddled over and picked it up. He stood there for a moment staring at me and then unfolded his wings and took off again. I gave the other pieces to Harry.

'I thought I wouldn't see him again. It's a sign.'

'What sort of sign?'

'Even Herbert's turning up for Christmas. You've got to keep asking Nick.'

'Hmm. I'm not sure I take relationship advice from herring gulls, but I'll think about it.'

He poured me a cup of tea.

'Drink up. We're leaving in five minutes.'

Herbert's appearance had raised my spirits and my anticipation rose on the short drive from Seacastle to the garden centre at Findon. As we passed the signpost to the Cissbury Ring, I vowed to visit it again before too long. We drove into the car park at the centre and stopped in front of a small stand of Christmas trees in various states of repair. One had already shed most of its leaves and another had a gap in its branches but there were a couple of stout examples with bushy branches and an excellent shape. Harry wanted to take the tallest but even I could tell we would be forced to cut the top off, spoiling the shape. I shook my head at him and pointed at the other bushy one which had its own pot.

'Are you sure?' said Harry. 'If you take the tag and pay at the cash register, I'll get it into the van.'

I went into the centre past a stand containing rows of poinsettia plants. I stopped to admire their bright red leaves with tiny flowers at the centre. A memory of my mother wiping the leaves of our Christmas poinsettia flooded my heart with feelings of longing. I picked two up and took them to the desk with me.

Harry raised his eyebrows as I walked back to the van, balancing one pot on each hand.

'Was it buy one, get one free?' he said. 'Or did they come with the tree?'

'Weren't you complaining about my lack of Christmas spirit earlier?'

'The way I remember it, I was complaining about you taking advice from a seagull. Hand them over.'

Mouse couldn't contain himself when he saw the tree and the poinsettias.

'Why didn't we do this last year? It's going to be fantastic. I've brought the decorations down from the attic.'

'Those belonged to my parents. You'll probably need to buy new Christmas lights. I doubt they're still working.'

'We could always ask the Nuttalls if they have any spare sets,' said Harry.

'Hilarious. Did you find the angel for the top of the tree?'

Mouse rummaged in the boxes, taking out strands of silver and gold tinsel and boxes of baubles in different colours. Waves of nostalgia hit me as I recognised my mother's conservative taste being revealed after years hidden away. I felt as if he were unboxing my Christmas past. Finally, he took out the battered angel with her bent wings and tattered dress.

'You mean this one,' he said, waving it in the air.

'Be careful. That's a family heirloom. My father bought it for their first Christmas together after he married my mother.'

'Wow! So, it's vintage?' said Harry. 'Maybe you should sell it in the shop.'

He swerved away, laughing as I aimed a punch at his arm. Mouse handed it to me and I gazed at it, trying to straighten its twisted halo.

'I'll get the stepladder,' said Harry. 'You can put it on top of the tree right now.'

We all set to decorating straight away. I'm not the most artistic of people so I just hang things where there is space. Mouse and Harry were no better. To our mutual amazement, the coloured lights still worked, flashing on and off after being plugged in. We hung all the baubles up and decked the branches with tinsel. Mouse found an old spray can of artificial snow, but it had hardened inside and was no longer serviceable. Then we stood back and admired our handiwork.

'It's fantastic,' said Harry. 'I'll take a photograph and send it to Nick.'

'Is he coming?' said Mouse. 'I'd love to meet him.'

'Maybe,' I said. 'He hasn't decided yet.'

Mouse rolled his eyes.

'It's not as if he's got anything better to do.'

'The tree might persuade him if you and Tanya stand underneath it with a sign.'

Five minutes later we stood under the tree with a coloured sign printed by Mouse from the computer. It had sprigs of holly on it and it said 'Please Come'. Harry needed a few goes to get us all into a selfie with the tree. Mouse took the phone from Harry and balanced it on a cupboard with the timer on. The resulting photo was wonderful and Harry sent it to Nick immediately. When Nick did not reply, disappointment was written all over his face. Mouse distracted him by pouring us all a glass of wine and making cheese on toast with tomato soup for supper, but I could sense him brooding. Some people just want to be alone at Christmas, but I didn't tell Harry that.

Chapter 11

The next morning, I showered and dressed full of the joys of the season. I asked Alexa to play Christmas music and bopped to Slade while I put my makeup on in the bathroom. Not a simple thing to do. Harry shook his head at me as he spread shaving foam onto his chin.

'What happened to the Grinch of Grotty Hovel? She has morphed into one of Santa's elves overnight.'

'I'm infected with tinselitis.'

'Hopeful you can't sing with that.'

'Are you being rude about my singing?'

'I can't talk. I'm shaving.'

I narrowed my eyes and patted blusher onto my cheeks until I got the effect I required. Then I bounced down the stairs, humming to the music. The dreadful scene that greeted me made me stop on the stair with my mouth open in shock. Harry came out to see why I had gone silent. He glanced into the sitting room and swore under his breath.

'What on earth has Hades done now? It's catageddon,' said Harry.

'I told you I heard something last night,' I said. 'But this is way worse than anything I could have possibly imagined.'

The Christmas tree had fallen into the middle of the room, scattering baubles everywhere. Several of them had shattered. Both poinsettias were lying on the floor, their roots exposed by the evacuation of the soil from their pots. One had broken in half. A sob rose in my throat as I picked my way through the carnage. I spotted Hades near the crown of the tree. He was washing himself without a care in the world. At his feet were the remains of my Christmas angel, destroyed by his sharp claws. I felt my blood boil, and I rushed at him. I aimed an air kick to frighten him, which threw me off balance and I fell against the Lloyd Loom laundry basket he used as his base. It collapsed under me as I landed, the supports splintering under my weight.

I sat on the floor and cursed and shouted at Hades who fled out through the cat flap. I staggered to my feet and followed him outside, screaming and flinging the empty poinsettia pot in his general direction. Then the pain of my fall overcame my fury, and I sank to the floor, sobbing. Harry, who had been transfixed by my furious reaction, came running downstairs and gathered me up in his arms. He carried me to the sofa where I wept a torrent of bitter tears. Harry picked up the angel and examined what was left of it. He shook his head at me. I held out my hand, and he placed the shredded mess in my palm.

'How could he?' I said. 'How could he do this to me after all I've done for him? I never want to see that cat again. Lock the cat flap. Now.'

Mouse appeared bleary eyed at the top of the stairs. His eyes opened wide as he took in the chaos.

'What happened?' he asked.

'Hades,' said Harry.

'He destroyed Christmas,' I said. 'I never want to see him again. If he comes back, take him to the vet and see who he really belongs to. They're welcome to him.'

'You don't mean that. Hades doesn't know any better. He's just a cat,' said Harry.

'He's evil, and he has always hated me. I'm the idiot that rescued him and fed him premium cat food. He sucked up to everyone except me. Do you realise he's never let me stroke him? Never. All he's ever done is scratch me. I'm not changing my mind. I hate him.'

I sobbed my heart out on the sofa, wrapped in a fleecy blanket while Mouse and Harry cleaned up the mess. I fell asleep eventually, exhausted by my tantrum. When I woke, the house was empty except for me and Hades. He sat on the floor in front of me without a care in the world. I couldn't believe he had the cheek to come into my house again. I jumped up and started screaming at him. He scrambled around the room with me chasing him until he exited through the cat flap. I went straight to the tool cupboard and took out a hammer and some nails. The cat flap was easy to nail shut. I made sure he couldn't lift it before I put away the tools. Then I went upstairs and hid under the duvet. It didn't take me long to fall into a deep sleep. At one stage, Hades yowling at the door downstairs penetrated my rest, but I didn't get up to let him in.

Hours later, Harry woke me by shaking my shoulder. Outside, the streetlights had come on, bathing the room in yellow light. I blinked and stretched. He stroked my face.

'Come downstairs, sweetheart.'

I shook my head.

'I don't want to.'

'Please. Just for a minute.'

I threw off the covers and stuck my feet in my slippers. I put my hair in a bun without brushing it. My reflection in the mirror gave me a fright. Red, puffy eyes stared back at me, making me wince. I came down the stairs slowly, uncertain of what I would find. To my surprise, the tree and the poinsettias had been restored to their former glory and a new set of snowflake lights twinkled along the bannisters. New decorations mingled with the remainder of the undamaged baubles hanging from the tree, heavily influenced by Mouse's taste. Star Wars figures and snowmen dangled together. There was even a Death Star. It looked quirky and wonderful. I tried to avoid looking at the top of the tree, but finally I glanced up. To my relief, they had not replaced my angel. The top of the tree was bare.

'I thought you could choose a new ornament,' said Harry, his voice catching in his throat. 'One for our tree, our Christmases to come.'

I couldn't speak. Mouse gave me a hug and Harry joined in. All my anger melted away.

'I'm sorry about the angel,' said Mouse. 'Hades didn't do it on purpose. He's just a cat. They know nothing about nostalgia.'

I looked around, but Hades's Lloyd Loom basket had gone.

'You smashed it,' said Harry. 'I've put it in the shed. Nick might fix it. He's handy.'

'Is he coming?' I asked.

'I haven't heard from him yet. He'll break eventually.'

'Where's Hades? I—'

My hand flew to my mouth as I remembered my fury.

'Oh no, I was so annoyed I nailed his door shut. I could hear him yowling when I was upstairs. Can you open it again?'

'Already done,' said Harry.

'But where is he?' I said.

'Sulking, I expect.'

'He'll come home when he's hungry,' said Mouse.

But he didn't.

Chapter 12

There was still no sign of Hades when I set out for the shop the next morning. I tried to rationalise his absence without making it my fault, but I failed. I had been too ashamed of my overreaction to tell Harry or Mouse how I had screamed at Hades when he came back inside and chased him out of the house. Remorse gripped my heart and squeezed it hard. Surely he would come home. Who else would buy premium cat food for a stray? I refused to feel guilty when he had provoked me. When I called to tell her about the angel's demise, Helen took my side for once. She even sniffled.

'Hades has no manners. He's an alley cat. But he should have known better than to destroy a bit of our legacy. Mum would be devastated.'

Helen was right. Our parents were dry sticks with Victorian values, but we missed them and their comments about the squander bug and the youth of today. They would not have approved of Hades and his spoilt ways. "Not one jot". I heard the voice of my father in my head as I walked along the promenade. The chill in the air hinted at colder days ahead, but I was not foolish enough to hope for a white Christmas. Snow at the seaside is not a common phenomenon, and it doesn't last long on the salty pavements. I didn't fancy slogging through slush.

I pulled my woolly hat down over my ears as the sea breeze followed me towards the theatre, whipping stray locks of my hair into the air. The tide had gone out and the pebble banks gave way to sandy patches interspersed with rock pools. Some hardy souls were walking their dogs on the tide line, slinging balls parallel to the water's edge and encouraging them to fetch the missiles before the sea stole them. Overhead, the seagulls wheeled and dived, keeping an eye out for any human approaching with a bag full of stale bread and burnt toast. I had a piece of toast in my pocket for Herbert, but I had no intention of giving it to one of his brethren.

The wind blew me up the side street to the door of Second Home and I had to push it shut behind me. I set to work removing extra lampshades from their boxes to place around the shop at eye level. I tagged them with clear prices, easily spotted from afar. As I had predicted, they were popular presents and the wide variety of colours meant that most people could pick one they liked. I drifted around the shop, dusting and rearranging, bringing articles out from the back and placing them in prominent spots. All those early mornings scouring boot sales for the most quirky and fashionable ephemera had been worth it. I loved my shop at that moment. It had saved me when I had nothing left after the divorce and brought me the gift of Harry.

Roz burst into the shop with Ghita. They were both rosy-cheeked with the cold.

'Ghita has volunteered to steer the ship while we go to the Veterans' Club and do some sleuthing,' said Roz. 'Are you ready, Jessica?'

They loved to compare me to Jessica Fletcher of Murder She Wrote, but I felt more like Morse that day; grumpy and hungover. I had to stop drinking so much wine because drinking and aging are opposites. One goes up and another goes down. The older you get, the less you can drink without feeling appalling. Some of us take longer than others to learn this life lesson.

'What's wrong with you?' said Ghita. 'You look as if someone shot your dog.'

'I'll tell you later, I promise. Do you fancy a chocolate éclair? We can get some in the Co-op on our way back.'

'I can resist everything except temptation.'

'Excellent. Mouse should be here to help you shortly, and we'll be back as soon as we can.'

The Veterans' Club occupied the first floor of a closed-down fancy furniture shop in a side street off the High Street. I never understood the point of having such a high-end shop in Seacastle. If they had hung on a little longer, they might have profited from the influx of new residents, but they had lasted about six months, a casualty of their optimism. We climbed the stairs and pushed our way through the swinging door into the club's small reception area. Roz pressed a buzzer on the desk and Violet Kent came out. She beamed at me and raised an eyebrow at Roz, who smiled at her.

'I've been expecting you,' she said to me, ignoring Roz. 'I took the visitors' logs out of storage in case you could find any useful information in them. Come through and I'll get them for you.'

She headed back through the door, holding it open for me. I turned to look at Roz who winked and shrugged. Another untold story. Roz had history with many people because of her inability to keep her nose out of other people's business. The centre consisted of two large rooms, one of which had a large television on the wall. The other had a trestle table with the scattered remains of various craft projects. An old man, bent over with osteoporosis, looked up from his knitting and smiled at us as we peered into the room.

'Why don't you sit at the table and I'll bring the visitors' books for you to look at?' said Violet.

We sat at the far end and waited for her to come back. I watched fascinated, as the old man's needles clicked and flicked as he knitted rows at impressive speed.

'It's a blanket for my dog,' he said. 'She's got arthritis.'

'I love the colour,' said Roz. 'Would you knit one for me?'

He stopped and put his head to one side.

'Are you just flirting or do you really want a blanket? You'll have to pay for the wool if you're serious.'

'I have a whole sack of wool at home that I got at a clearance,' I said. 'You're welcome to it.'

'Really? I'd love that,' said the man. 'Can you bring it here?'

'Roz will bring it, and she can negotiate with you over the blanket. Her husband is a fisherman. Maybe you can barter and get some fresh seafood for it.'

'It's a deal. My name's Derrick Magee, by the way.'

'I'm Tanya.'

Violet Kent bustled back into the room carrying a couple of large ledgers. She huffed and puffed as she laid them on the table.

'These are from the right era,' she said.

Derrick's expression changed like a black cloud rumbling over a beach and blocking out the sun. His brow furrowed, and he bowed his head to his knitting. I could tell he had something to say by the way he muttered to himself. I waited for Violet to leave before opening the first ledger and leafing through it. I soon found an instance of Gladys's signature and then one from Cyril Prout. At first, the distribution seemed random, but I remember the movie nights and concentrated on Saturdays.

'Look,' said Roz. 'Both of them on the same night.'

Sure enough, their name and signatures were entered below a heading saying Movie Night.

'That's the night they met. Seven years ago.'

'She planned it,' said Derrick, dropping his knitting on the table.

We both stared at him in amazement. He shrugged.

'You're that investigator, aren't you? I recognise you from the telly. And I read about poor old Cyril being found in a garden.'

Roz laughed.

'I think you've got competition, Tan.'

'Did you know Cyril?' I asked.

'Aye. I knew Gladys too, hussy.'

'That's harsh. Why are you calling her names?'

'She were mine until that Cyril Prout turned up. She dumped me like a hot coal when she found out he were loaded.'

'Loaded?'

'He owned that house on Keat's Road, dint he? Mortgage free. That's loaded compared to most of us veterans. I couldn't compete.'

He shuffled his dentures around his mouth and picked up his knitting to signify the conversation was over. Roz elbowed me sharply in the ribs and pointed at the doorway. I shook my head.

'Wait,' I hissed.

I continued to leaf through the register while Roz fidgeted beside me. Finally, she stood up.

'I'll see you outside,' she said. 'I've got to check something.'

As Derrick watched me writing in my notebook, he relaxed again with the rhythm of his clicking needles. I realised I could ask him some more questions.

'Did Cyril tell you about his planned trip to Turkey?' I asked.

He shook his head.

'No. He mentioned nowt about going there. He would've told me about it. Who told you Cyril went to Turkey? They were lying. They must have killed him.'

He had a point. Was Gladys covering her tracks by inventing Cyril's holiday? I couldn't imagine what motive she had. After all, the house next door to Grotty Hovel didn't belong to her as far as I knew. It had been turned into a guesthouse by its owner. But who were they, and how did they end up with Cyril's house? Derrick had mentioned the house as a motive for murder, and he was right. If Cyril had disappeared near to the time I moved into the Grotty Hovel, who had ordered the house clearance? I met Harry for the first time when he did a clearance of Cyril's house. He kept records of all his clients, so he should have a contact number of the owner. I looked down at the logbook again. This job was more complex than I had imagined. I needed Mouse to work his magic on it and track the people who were at the club when Cyril was. Who saw him last? Could the information be written in the register?

Derrick had not only raised some important points with me. He had also put himself in the frame for murder. He still harboured fury over Gladys deserting him for Cyril. Caving in a man's skull with a blunt object seemed to me to need strength and passion. Could Derrick have taken out his jealousy on Cyril, and buried him in the Grotty Hovel's back garden? He could easily have used Cyril's phone to send fake messages to Gladys to put her off the trail. Gladys struck me as a stubborn person. She would have investigated Cyril's disappearance if she had had doubts about the fake trip to Turkey. Whoever had taken Cyril's cell phone after his death would have got rid of it years ago.

I had to speak to Harry and Mouse before I could get any further with the investigation. Mouse would be far better than me at organising the data from the Veterans' Club register. I almost knocked over my chair in my haste to leave. Derrick sucked his teeth and watched me go.

'Thanks for your help,' I said. 'I'll look into your allegations. Do you come here often?'

'I would if I thought you might be here,' he said, leering at me.

He'd be waiting a long time in that case. I shuddered and backed out of the room.

'Did you get what you were after?' said Violet, as I came through the door into reception.

'Not exactly. I wondered if you could leave the books out for my son. He's a bit of a whizz with computers and I'd like him to make a table of the comings and goings, if that's okay with you.'

'I don't mind. Nothing exciting ever happens here. It will be a breath of fresh air to have a young man about the place. Can he bring me a piece of cake from your café? I've heard great things about the Christmas cherry one.'

'Of course. I'm on my way there now. He'll be here soon.'

I descended the steps into the street to find Roz still there, hopping from foot to foot in impatience.

'Why did you take so long?' she said. 'I've had an idea, and it's brilliant. I even made a call—'

'Can it wait until we get to the shop? I need coffee before any new ideas.'

She sighed and shrugged.

'Okay. I bought the éclairs already. Let's go to Second Home.'

Chapter 13

I hardly noticed the walk back to Second Home. My head swam with suspects and motives. Could Gladys be lying to us? I had really taken to her and I couldn't bear to imagine her plotting to kill Cyril for his house. Didn't she already own her flat? I had assumed she did, much as I had taken her at face value. But a murderer? There had to be more to this story, but my brain wouldn't cooperate. We got to the shop after a brisk walk. Roz chuntered all the way, desperate to tell me her news, but I pretended not to notice. Sometimes I needed fewer facts to work out a case, not more.

Mouse waited for us at the cash desk of the shop, his brow furrowed.

'You took your time,' he said. 'Ghita told me you would be right back.'

'Where's the fire?' I asked, looking around. 'We're not exactly busy.'

'It's Hades. He didn't come home. I've looked everywhere. He's missing and I can't find him.'

His voice broke with distress. A wave of guilt ran through my veins. Had I scared Hades away for ever? Mouse would never forgive me if he found out what I had done. Even more to the point, I would never forgive myself if Hades didn't return. I put my arm around his shoulders.

'I'm sorry about Hades, but I need you to search the register in the Veterans' Club and find out who Cyril saw the last few times he visited. Maybe it will narrow down the field of suspects.'

'But I can't just abandon Hades. Something has happened to him.'

'I can look for Hades. I'll knock on the doors of the neighbours and see if anybody is feeding him. It will give me a good excuse to do some sleuthing about the murder of Cyril Prout.'

'What if he has gone away or got lost?'

'Why don't you make a poster and stick it on the lamp posts of the streets in our part of town? I noticed the club had a large printer. You could ask Violet to help you by printing some out.'

'Why would she help me?'

'Sweetheart, you really need to look in the mirror one of these days. She'll help if you ask politely. Bring her a big slice of cherry cake and a nice latte. Perhaps a few of Ghita's almond biscuits too.'

'Will you try to find Hades? It won't be Christmas without him.'

'I'll leave shortly, I promise.'

He shook his head.

'No, I want you to go now. Then I'll collect that information from the Veterans' Club for you.'

'If Ghita and Roz don't mind,' I said.

'I do,' said Roz.

Ghita kicked her in the shin.

'We'll be fine,' she said. 'Go.'

'I'll be back as soon as I can.'

'What about my news?' said Roz.

'It will keep,' said Ghita. 'Get out of here, Tan. I can't bear to see our Mouse so upset.'

'A Mouse upset about a cat. That's a first,' said Roz.

'Thanks girls. See you shortly.'

I tried not to fret about Hades on my way home, but his disappearance added another layer of worry to my already frazzled nerves. I left my car outside the Grotty Hovel and walked to the first house on the other side of the street, going on the principle that people who lived across the street from him were more likely to have had a clear view of the goings on at Cyril's house. The residents of Keat's Road were mostly older retired people, often from London and the Southeast. In years gone by, we would have all known each other, but I felt nervous about knocking on the doors of people I had never met. Hades had given me a fortuitous excuse. I felt sure he would be lounging on somebody's couch glaring at me, but how I would remove him was a conundrum I couldn't solve.

Nobody came to the door at number two when I rang the doorbell. It was the same story at number four, six and eight. I saw a curtain twitch at number ten, but the door remained closed. I knocked instead, waiting. Finally, the door opened on a chain. A cross face appeared in the gloom.

'What do you want? I'm not buying anything.'

'I'm not selling anything. My cat is missing.'

'And you think I've got it? Piss off.'

She slammed the door in my face. Not a good start. I went next door. No answer. The same with number fourteen. I almost lost heart. When I rang the doorbell on number sixteen, the door opened immediately, almost as if the occupant had placed themselves behind it, anticipating my arrival. It caught me so unawares I almost fell inside. A tiny old lady with twinkly eyes who reminded me a little of Gladys stood on the threshold looking up at me.

'Alright, lovey?' said the woman. 'You're as popular as a dose of salts around here from what I can see. What are you selling?'

'Nothing. I'm looking for our cat, Hades. He's gone missing.'

'Your cat? What colour is he?'

'He's black with a white bib.'

'Why are you looking on this street?'

'I live here. In number thirty-three.'

'When did you move in?'

'A couple of years ago. My ex-husband bought the house from Shawn Denny.'

'That shyster. He got his paws on it after Daphne Sands died.'

'Did you know Daphne? I've met her daughter.'

'We went to school together. Her daughter didn't associate with the likes of me. She left home at sixteen and never came back.'

'What happened to Daphne?'

'She had a fall, I think. I'm fuzzy on the details, but they say she was pushed.'

I did a double take.

'Who says?'

'That would be telling. But it's only a rumour, and I don't believe it anyway. Cyril's actually dead, isn't he?'

'Did you know Cyril Prout?'

Her face fell.

'That poor man. They found him in your garden, didn't they? I'm not surprised your cat ran away.'

'Oh, no. He didn't run away then. Although I suppose he could have been affected by it. We all are.'

'Do they know what happened to Cyril?'

'I'm afraid they think somebody murdered him.'

'Murder? So soon after Daphne died? That's horrific.'

'How do you know he died soon after Daphne?'

'I saw you moving in to Daphne's house, when they emptied Cyril's house.'

'That's when we got our cat. He was trapped in a basket in the sitting room.'

'Oh, that cat. He was feral. He'd go missing for months. Cyril just disappeared you know. I only knew he had gone when your boyfriend emptied his house.'

'Harry? That's when I met him you know.'

She raised an eyebrow.

'That's some coincidence.'

I could imagine the cogs whirling in her head.

'My husband announced he was divorcing me out of the blue. He bought number thirty-three and gave me the keys as part of the settlement. I had no choice. And Harry's the best thing that ever happened to me. We have nothing to do with the murders.'

'Murders? I thought only Cyril was murdered.'

'That's what I meant.'

But her brain wasn't the only one that was whirring. What if Daphne's death could be linked to Cyril's?

'I'd better keep going,' I said. 'My son is distressed about our cat going missing. I promised him I'd keep looking.'

'If I were you, I'd keep a close eye on your loved ones. Those houses are bad luck. What if the killings haven't stopped?'

'You haven't told me your name.'

'Betty Staples. And yours?'

'Tanya Bowe. It's been interesting to meet you.'

She laughed.

'And you. Good luck with your search for the cat. If I see him, I'll bring him home for you.'

Chapter 14

I knocked on every door on that side of the street. Many houses were empty in the afternoon because their inhabitants were out shopping or working. Nobody I found at home had seen Hades, but several people had strong opinions on the goings on at thirty-three and thirty-one Keat's Road. It seemed to me the police had been totally disinterested in the death of Daphne Sands and were far too quick to ascribe it to accidental causes. Shades of Melanie Conrad and the initial verdict of death by misadventure. I wondered if their apathy was linked to the age of the victims. Maybe George would let me see Daphne's autopsy result. Since I was helping him unofficially on the Cyril Prout case, I could see him being more willing than usual if he thought I might help him clear it up before Christmas.

I let myself into the house and spent an hour writing up my notes for each house. Then I foraged in the fridge for the ingredients to make bubble and squeak to have with the cold lamb leftovers from our Sunday joint. While I was cutting the maximum amount of meat I could salvage from the shoulder bone, the door opened and Mouse let himself in. He wandered over to the table and read my notes.

'What are these?' he said. 'I thought you were looking for Hades.'

'Oh, I was. But I took advantage of having them on the doorstep to ask questions about Cyril.'

His brow furrowed.

'Why did you go across the road if you were looking for Hades? Surely, it would have made more sense to stay on our side? Hades would have run into other people's gardens from ours.'

I had no answer to this. He sighed.

'I can't believe it. You're so obsessed with this stupid investigation, as usual. You don't care about Hades at all.'

'I'm sorry. I got carried away, but it seems like the former owner of this house may also have died under suspicious circumstances. Do you think I should ignore their deaths just because they're old and our cat has gone missing?'

'How am I supposed to know that? That's not a fair question.'

'I know it isn't. I really am sorry. Hades is a special cat and I promise to do this side of the road tomorrow. You shouldn't worry about him. He is probably lying on someone's sofa and eating tasty titbits.'

'I suppose so.'

'Did you make the posters?'

'Yes. I've got them here.'

'Why don't we take a roll of masking tape and stick them on the lamp posts on this and the two parallel roads? There's time before supper.'

He nodded sulkily at me. I rolled my eyes inwardly. Hades and Mouse had been like two peas in a pod from the day Mouse first broke into my house and made himself at home. Hades had definitely missed Mouse while he had been at university. He slept on Mouse's bed nearly every night as if waiting for him to return. I had never had more than a grudging pat and only got attention from Hades when he felt hungry, so our bond was much looser. I missed Hades though, a lot more than I expected. I covered the meat and put it in the fridge. It would've been just like Hades to reappear and gobble down our supper.

I put on my coat and scarf and we headed out with the tape and the posters. Mouse soon recovered his good humour as we stuck the posters on lamp posts and fences. We met several people on our travels who all promised to keep an eye out for him too. By the time we got home again, all was forgiven. I headed for the kitchen to fry up the bubble and squeak while Mouse laid the table. Harry came in not long after, carrying a bottle of wine he had picked up at the off licence.

'I'm home,' he said. 'What's for supper? I'm starving.'

'Cold lamb with bubble and squeak,' I said.

'Delicious. Shall I pour us all a glass of vino?'

'Yes, please. Before you do that, I need a favour.'

'Before the wine. Okay.'

He sighed theatrically.

'Do you remember the day we met?' I asked.

'Best day of my life.'

'And mine. But who paid you to do the clearance next door? I remember a plump woman in a suit who almost fell out of her car in her haste to give you the keys. I need you to search your records and find out who she was.'

'I'm not sure she had anything to do with it, besides giving me the keys to the house. A property company hired me, I think. I can look it up, but I'd prefer to do it after supper.'

'Fair enough. Pour the wine. Supper's almost ready.'

After a delicious meal, Harry went through the cardboard box known as his 'office'. I had offered to let him share my vintage filing cabinet, but he preferred his box.

'I'll swap it for a new one if it gets too tattered,' he said.

He bent over the box and shuffled the contents around, grunting with effort.

'Does it have to be now? My stomach is bursting.'

'Yes, it does.'

More grunting. Then he straightened up and waved a battered logbook in his hand.

'I knew it was here. I only finished it recently.'

He plonked himself down on the sofa and flicked back through the pages, scratching his head.

'Aha. Here it is. Clearance of thirty-one Keat's Road. Client is Beach Holdings Ltd.'

'Do they have an address or a phone number?'

'None that I can see.'

'How about the woman in the suit?' said Mouse. 'Have you got a name for her?'

'I can't read my writing. Magee perhaps. No first name or number, though. Can't you look it up on the net, Mouse?'

'There's not a whole load to go on, but I'll have a search,' said Mouse. 'Not tonight, though. I want to watch a movie. How about you?'

'No thanks,' I said. 'I'm going to read my notes again. We're missing something vital, but I have no idea what it is.'

'Hades,' said Mouse. 'That's what's missing.'

'Wait a minute. Isn't that the surname of the man at the Veterans' Club?'

'Which man?'

'Hang on.'

I read my notes from my visit to the club and gasped.

'I met a man called Derrick Magee. A nasty piece of work. He told me Cyril had stolen Gladys from him. He claimed she wanted to get her hands on Cyril's house, but what if he was the one who wanted Cyril's property?'

'Maybe you should tell George about him?' said Harry.

'Then you can keep looking for Hades instead,' said Mouse.

I squirmed, but they were staring me down. I muttered to myself, but I pulled out my phone and dialled George's number.

'Hi Tan. Did you find out anything at the Veterans' Club?'

'I did. There's a man called Derrick Magee who frequents the place. He claimed Cyril stole Gladys from him.'

'That's not much to go on.'

'I thought you'd say that, but it's possible he hired Harry to do the clearance of Cyril's house. Harry has a note about someone called Magee arranging to give him the keys.'

'That sounds promising. Leave it with me. I'll let you know if we dig up anything.'

He hung up. I felt a sulk coming on, but Mouse gave me a hug.

'I'll go to Second Home and open it up tomorrow morning,' he said. 'If you promise to keep looking for Hades.'

'It's a deal. I'll do this side of the road before I come to work.'

Chapter 15

After Mouse and Harry had left the next morning, I dutifully returned to the doorsteps of Keat's Road to find out if anyone had seen Hades. Several occupants almost bowled me over on their way out to work, shaking their heads when asked if they had seen a black cat with a white bib. I thought it likely they were telling the truth, since they would have been out working at the time Hades fled the Grotty Hovel for good. He most likely sought refuge with somebody who worked from home or was retired and was always in. I also wanted to find out more about Cyril Prout from his neighbours, if I could, despite risking the wrath of Mouse.

As had happened on the other side of our street, most of the houses had no occupants after nine o'clock, but the old lady in the house next door to us came out to greet me with a big smile. I recognised her from Cyril's funeral.

'I wondered when you'd get around to visiting me. Betty from across the way told me you'd been asking questions about Daphne and Cyril.'

'She was so helpful,' I said. 'I feel as if I'm a terrible neighbour. I've been here nearly two years and I haven't made friends with anyone on the street yet.'

'You may not know us, but we know you and your partner. If I had a man like that, I wouldn't come outside often either,' she said, winking. 'My name's Irene

Handley. I've lived on the street for twenty years, and I'm as nosy as Betty Staples.'

Her eyes twinkled in her lively face as she said this. I felt as if I had discovered a hidden stratum of society comprising dangerous old ladies who hunted gossip in packs. I decided to invite them all to the café or the Grotty Hovel so they could meet Gladys and plot world domination. I grinned.

'Harry is rather scrumptious, but I'm not here about him. Have you seen our cat, Hades? He's gone missing. He's large and black with a white bib.'

'Hades? The name suits him. I've seen him often. He stalks along the top of the brick wall at the back of the gardens. He's a ferocious hunter. But not in the last few days.'

I sighed.

'My son is missing him terribly. Please can you keep an eye out for us?'

'Of course. Aren't you going to ask me about Daphne? She was one of our crew, you know. We all hung out together for years and years.'

I had intended to question her about Cyril, but instead I commented, 'It must have been dreadful for you all when she died.'

Her eyes clouded with tears as she fought for an answer.

'You can't imagine how we felt. Especially the way she died. We didn't believe it was an accident, but nobody listens to us.'

'What do you mean?'

'She had twisted her ankle the week before her death, so she couldn't walk more than a few steps. We had been helping her with the shopping and so on.'

'That was nice of you.'

'Just being neighbourly. Anyway, she had been sleeping downstairs on the sofa, because she couldn't go up to her bedroom.'

'But didn't the police report that she had fallen downstairs?'

'They claimed she must have hobbled up to get something and fallen back down the steps. But she would have asked us to help her. She used to bang on the wall with her broom handle if she wanted me to get her something from upstairs. But the police wouldn't listen. You'll realise as you get older, people look right through you like you don't matter anymore.'

She sniffed.

'Do you think somebody murdered her?'

'I'm sure someone attacked her. I don't know whether they intended to kill her, but when Cyril disappeared so soon afterwards, we were worried he had something to do with it.'

'But why would Cyril have hurt Daphne?'

'She stalked him for years. The poor man never had a moment's peace. We wondered if he had lost his temper and hit her over the head with something.'

'And now?'

'We don't know what to think. I mean. Who died first? Did someone kill Daphne because she saw them burying Cyril in their garden? Or vice-versa.'

'The timing is crucial isn't it, if I want to solve the mystery?'

Irene's eyes opened wide and her mouth fell open.

'Oh my giddy aunt! I thought I recognised you. You're her, aren't you? I can't believe it.'

I smiled.

'Yes, I was Tanya Carter from Uncovering the Truth, but I'm now Tanya Bowe again and I interfere in my ex-husband's murder cases.'

'Is that a revenge thing?'

I laughed.

'No. We actually get on pretty well, but I guess you already know that.'

'We've been gossiping about the two of you ever since you moved into Keat's Road. At one stage, we thought you might get back together, but we prefer your new man. He's right up our street.'

She roared with laughter at my expression.

'We're old, dearie, but we're not dead yet,' she said. 'Have the police got any leads on who killed Cyril yet?'

'I don't think so. They're short staffed with Christmas coming up. That's why I'm helping in an unofficial capacity.'

'If I were you, I'd be investigating the ownership of Cyril's house. Somebody had it cleared soon after he disappeared and then let it out as an Airbnb with new furniture. They would have needed instructions from him to do those things.'

'Weirdly, I met Harry when he did the clearance of Cyril's house. So, we have the name of the company who ordered it. My stepson, Mouse, is going to investigate that for me today.'

'He's the young man who lives with you? Oh my, he's a heartbreaker, isn't he? We haven't seen much of him recently.'

'Mouse is at university studying Forensic Computing. He's a skilled hacker, but we're trying to encourage him to work for the good guys. He's just returned for the Christmas holidays.'

'Will you let us know how the investigation is going? We're so thrilled somebody is finally doing something about Daphne. She was a stubborn old stick, but she had a good heart. It's a pity Cyril preferred Gladys, but that's love, isn't it?'

By the time I had knocked on every door, I felt exhausted and thought about popping home for a coffee.

Instead, I took out my phone and texted Helen and invited myself to her house, which was on a parallel road a couple of streets away. Soon I was sitting in her front room sipping a nice mug of filter coffee.

'I haven't apologised for being grumpy about my garden,' I said. 'I know you organised it as a kindness.'

She snorted with laughter.

'What I did was give you a murder investigation for Christmas. George is livid, poor lamb.'

'You couldn't have organised a better present. I'm loving it. I know I shouldn't, but I'm in my element. And Gladys deserves to know what happened to the love of her life. That's my present for her.'

'Have you found Hades yet?'

'No. Mouse is devastated, but we put up some posters yesterday.'

'I saw them this morning when I went to buy some milk in the corner shop. They're so cute. I'm just afraid whoever has him won't want to give him back.'

'Wait until he pulls down their Christmas tree. They'll go off him quickly.'

'You have a point.'

'By the way, do you have the name of the agency who let the house beside the Grotty Hovel to you, when you came to the tribute competition with Olivia? I wanted to ask them some questions.'

'I've got the contract in my desk somewhere. Do you want it now?'

'If you can find it. I think they might be key to finding out what happened to Cyril.'

'Give me a minute.'

I waited patiently while she pulled out a folder and leafed through the papers.

'Yes, here it is. Do you want to make a copy and give it back to me?'

'Excellent. I will solve this mystery before Christmas if it kills me.'

'And find Hades before Mouse dissolves into misery?'

'He's out there somewhere.'

'Have you tried asking the vet if they have him registered? If someone hands him in, they will contact you.'

'I'm afraid they might contact his actual owner.'

'Isn't he dead?'

'Good point. I'll get Mouse to tell the vet that Hades is now ours.'

'I'm looking forward to Christmas. It will be nice to all be together for once. Some people just aren't that lucky.'

And that's when I considered enlarging the table…

Chapter 16

I dropped into the Grotty Hovel on my way to work and copied Helen's contract, which I stuffed into my handbag. It had started to rain by the time I came out again, so I jumped into the Mini and drove to Second Home. It took ages to find a parking space, and I had forgotten my umbrella, so I was soggy and grumpy by the time I entered the shop. Roz and Ghita were serving a gaggle of customers who appeared to have come from a bus tour of some sort. The clients, mostly females, were peering into all the nooks and crannies of the shop and finding all the trinkets I had deployed for Christmas purchases. One of them alerted the group that we had a café upstairs and they all migrated there with cries of high excitement, carrying their treasures.

Ghita followed them upstairs to help Mouse serve them, leaving me downstairs with Roz.

'I see you've been busy without me,' I said.

'It's been manic this morning. People have suddenly decided Christmas is coming fast and begun to panic buy.'

'Fantastic. I'm sorry about deserting you yesterday. Hades is top priority for Mouse. He doesn't care about the murder as much.'

'I do. I haven't told you about my thought yet. Why don't you find out who owns the house now? If somebody is maintaining the fiction that Cyril is still alive, the house must still be in his name. But if someone sold it on his behalf, there must be proof of sale somewhere.'

'That's a great idea.'

I reached into my handbag.

'Look at this contract Helen signed to rent Cyril's house. Is the company who did the clearance, the same one who put the house on Airbnb? Who owns the company and how did they get permission for these actions?'

'Are you going to call them?'

'As soon as we deal with all these customers. Do we have enough milk for their coffees?'

'For the time being we do. Luckily, I just bought a couple of two litre bottles. I'll slip out and get some more if you hold the fort.'

'Perfect. Buy us some chocolate croissants in case the bus load clears us out of cake.'

It took nearly an hour before the last of the ladies had finished their coffee and sweet treats and paid for their treasures. Most of them paid with bank cards, but I also had a full cash register, not something that happened very often. I bundled up the cash and filled out a deposit form before sending Mouse down the road to the bank to deposit the cash for safety. Then we treated ourselves to a quick cuppa upstairs while the shop was quiet.

'Phew. Talk about rush hour,' said Ghita. 'There's only half a cake left, and I brought three freshly baked ones in yesterday. Do you mind if I go home and do some more baking? I have a feeling we could do with another batch as soon as possible. Plus, I've taken several orders for whole cakes, which I need to fill.'

'That's great news. Of course you can. We'll be okay here. If Roz will help me, I'd like to dig out more trinkets and treasures to scatter around the shop. Those ladies almost cleared us out, but I have several boxes full of miscellaneous goodies in the loft rooms.'

After Ghita and Mouse had left, Roz and I went upstairs to the loft and brought down four boxes which I had filled and stored there over the last few months. I loved to unpack these boxes. There were always forgotten curios and ornaments lurking amongst their contents. Roz unwrapped each one and showed it to me so I could give her a price to write on its label. She put a few items aside without asking for prices and I guessed they were gifts for her family and for Ed. I only charged her and Ghita at cost and often failed to ask them for the money. I could not afford to pay them much, so I was quite happy to let them have their hearts' desires cheap or free as a perk. We all drank free coffee, but I paid Ghita for every slice of cake and each almond biscuit we ate. Her business kept the Vintage buzzing, so I was determined to make sure it was worth her while to bake for me.

When we had finished unpacking the boxes, I retrieved Helen's contract from my handbag and called the contact number written on it. I didn't have to wait long for an answer.

'Shore Management. How may we assist you?'

Her voice sounded familiar. I didn't want her to recognise mine, so I pretended to drop the phone. I cut off the call and went downstairs to where Roz organised the last of the trinkets into their nooks.

'Can you make a call for me, please? I'm trying to arrange a meeting at the company managing Cyril's house, but I don't want the person on the other end to hear my voice.'

'Why not?'

'I think I recognise her voice but I can't place her.'

'Sure. What do you want me to say?'

I explained I needed her to ask for an appointment for letting out my house as an Airbnb.

'But tell her your husband will go to it as you are too busy.'

'Ed?'

'No. George. I'll tell him to interview her about Cyril's house.'

'Okay. Shall I redial the last number?'

'Yes, just tell her you're sorry for cutting off the call, but you dropped the phone when your dog jumped up at you.'

Roz sighed and held up her hand to silence me. She dialled the number and spoke to the woman, setting up a meeting for the next day. I racked my brains, but I couldn't place the voice of the woman who had spoken to me. How had I met her before? Was it on a clearance? Or was she a client of the shop?

'There you go,' said Roz. 'All sorted. I've tapped the address in with the entry for the phone number. You can send George the contact by text.'

'Thanks. I'll ring him now.'

George did not sound at all pleased when I called him.

'Your tip about Mr Magee turned out to be a complete wild goose chase. He became quite irate when I tried to question him. There isn't a scrap of evidence he killed Cyril Prout. He's in a wheelchair, you know.'

'Oh. I'd forgotten about him. I'm sorry. He was sitting down when I met him, so I didn't realise he was disabled.'

'Honestly, I looked like a prat. You need to be more careful.'

'Don't be cross with me. I've got a much better lead for you this time. Helen gave me the number of the company who let Cyril's house to her. I rang them up, well Roz did, because I thought I recognised the voice, and she made an appointment for you to talk to them.'

George sighed.

'Can I come over for a coffee? I need a piece of cake before I can grasp any of this.'

'Sure. I have some lovely presents Helen might like too.'

I could hear him sighing as he hung up.

Chapter 17

Hades did not turn up that evening, or the next. Poor Mouse spent fruitless hours knocking on doors in the streets parallel to ours, searching for him. He slumped into a chair on his return, his brow sweaty and his mouth down-turned. I could almost feel the hurt in his heart. Hades had given Mouse stability in his early days at the Grotty Hovel and somewhere to lavish all the repressed love he had been storing. Mouse had learned to love me, and Harry too now. Even his father George got some grudging affection. But Hades had his heart.

'No luck, sweetheart?' I said. 'I'm sure he'll turn up soon. You know he'll smell our turkey and come running.'

'Do you really think so?'

'I know so. Don't fret.'

'But I need to do something. All that is left of him are his collar and his bowl.'

'What collar? Wasn't he wearing it when he disappeared?'

'The one he had on when you found him.'

'Have you still got it?'

'It's in my room.'

'Have you ever looked closely at it?'

'Not really. I chucked it in a box when I cut it off. It was far too tight, remember?'

'Maybe we should have a look?'

Mouse jumped off the sofa and ran upstairs. I heard him throwing things around in his bedroom. Eventually, he came back downstairs, waving it in the air.

'It's got an inscription on it. I didn't see it before because it's almost worn flat. Where's your magnifying glass?'

'In the righthand drawer of the bureau. Let's have a look.'

Mouse handed me the collar and the magnifying glass and I held them in the light. The collar, worn and faded, had a small, barely legible engraving on the inside.

'To B, Love H.'

Mouse scratched his head.

'That doesn't help much. Nobody involved in the investigation has a name beginning with those letters.'

'Why don't you go to and see the vet tomorrow? You can ask him if any of the chips he inserted are registered to the Grotty Hovel or to Cyril's house. Maybe he can tell you who Hades belongs to?'

'But what if they want Hades back?'

I could swear I saw his bottom lip quiver. Mouse teetered on the verge of manhood, but often seemed unwilling to make the irrevocable step. Having finally found a family, he had no particular hurry to spread his wings. To tell you the truth, I treasured every minute of his elongated childhood. But another truth hovered on the edge of my consciousness. I put my hand to his face.

'Somebody owned Hades before us. What if they miss him as much as you do?'

He turned away.

'Why do you have to be so sensible? It's not fair.'

'I know, sweetheart, but if Hades belonged to Cyril or Daphne, we can keep him. Who knows where they got the collar. It looks quite old. Maybe it's an heirloom.'

'I guess so.'

'Everything will work out in the end.'

He gave me a hug and took the collar back to his room. He sat on his bed surfing the net until he got a call from a friend and left to go to a party. My soothing words did not work on me. A creeping feeling of guilt had wrapped its tendrils around my conscience, and I tossed and turned all night, driving Harry to despair. He sighed with relief when I got up the next morning.

'Honestly, it's like sleeping with a python on acid. Can't you take a tranquillizer or something?'

I ignored him, putting on my warm dressing gown and going downstairs to make tea. The doorbell rang while I waited for the kettle to boil. I thought it might be the postman with parcels for Christmas, but George stood there in his wool coat flecked with raindrops. I could almost imagine the damp smell.

'Aren't you going to invite me in?' he said, squinting as a raindrop fell on his eyelashes.

'Of course. Sorry, I'm half asleep. Tea?'

'Absolutely. Can we have toast too? Helen forgot to buy bread.'

'That's not like her. She's usually so efficient.'

'She's been under the weather recently.'

'I didn't notice.'

'You aren't very observant then.'

Totally untrue, but I didn't want a row. I wanted information. George had been to see the company who managed Cyril's house, but I hadn't heard from him since.

'What happened to you yesterday? I've been desperate to know what happened at your meeting.'

'Oh, yes. Sorry. I had to go to Brighton to work on an investigation with DI Antrim. We went for a pint after work and, well, you know how it is.'

I did. Actually, I was glad to hear George and Terry were getting on better. Their rivalry had morphed into a bromance when no one was looking. I beckoned him to the kitchen, putting my finger to my lips and pointed upstairs. He rolled his eyes and flung his coat on the sofa. I shut the kitchen door behind him and poured us a cuppa. Soon we were munching toast and marmalade and licking our fingers to catch the melted butter.

'Yum. I needed that,' said George. 'You can't beat warm buttered toast and marmalade.'

'Best meal of the day. Can you please put me out of my misery and tell me about your meeting at Shore Management?'

'After I arrived at their office, I didn't bother with the pretence of letting a house. I presented my credentials and started asking questions before the manager had time to cover her tracks. She seemed flabbergasted when I told her about Cyril Prout. She protested her innocence and showed me a letter she had on file, which she claimed to have received from Beach Management as proof of their right to let out the house. It's from Cyril Prout. He claims to be abroad and asks Beach Management to clear the house and get someone to manage letting it out. She said she administrated various properties for companies like that.'

'Seriously? Do you have it with you?'

'I sent the original in for finger printing, but I'm not sure how we'll know if any prints belong to Cyril.'

'What if they belong to someone else?'

'Unless they're in the system, we are unlikely to get a match. Maybe your pal Gladys has something with Cyril's fingerprints on it?'

'That's a good call. Can I have a copy of the letter? I'd like to show it to Gladys.'

He patted his jacket pocket.

'I've got one right here. Don't go showing it around town.'

'I won't. Just Gladys. I promise. By the way, what happens to the money from the rentals?'

'Helen says she deposited her payment into an account owned by Beach Holdings.'

'That's also the company who paid Harry to clear Cyril's house. But how did they acquire the property that's the question? How did they get a letter from Cyril if he was already dead? Don't you think something smells bad here? Shore Management and Beach Holdings sound remarkably similar.'

'It is weird, now that you mention it. When he bothers to get up, can you ask my son to put his hacking skills to good use and find out who the directors of both companies are, please? My computer people have gone on holiday already. I really don't know why we bother. Soon everyone will take the whole of December off.'

'I'll ask him. Don't forget to leave me the copy of the letter. I'll get Gladys in to look at it today.'

As George opened his mouth to speak, I heard the metal creak of our letter box and a letter dropped on the floor. I held up my finger to George and went to collect it.

'Can't it wait?'

'It might be money.'

He rolled his eyes at me. I picked up the envelope and examined it. Somebody had written my name on the front, but no address. Mystified, I unsealed it and skimmed the contents. They made me sink into my chair with my hand over my mouth.

'What does it say?' said George.

I handed it to him and he read it too. His eyebrows flew up.

'What the heck?'

He ran to the front door and gazed up and down the street before returning to the kitchen where I was re-reading the note in disbelief. Somebody had kidnapped Hades and was threatening to kill him if I didn't stop investigating the death of Cyril Prout. I couldn't take it in. Who would send such a macabre threat? George took the note from me again. He re-read it, puffing in exasperation.

'The cheek of it,' he said. 'In all my years as a police officer, I've never seen one of these. You've really stirred up a hornets' nest with this investigation.'

'Do you think it's true? Will they hurt Hades?'

'I have no idea, but we can't stop the investigation because of a cat.'

'A cat? That's your son's soulmate, not just any animal.'

George shook his head.

'I know, but I can't be sidetracked now. Maybe it would be better if you told me everything you know and let me get on with it in the background. You seem to be the centre of their attention. Perhaps if you pretend to have given up, they won't harm him.'

I could see the logic of it, even if I hated the idea. It was time to spill the beans about the former owner of the Grotty Hovel.

'Okay, but I have some new information about the Daphne Sands case that may be relevant.'

'Daphne Sands? That wasn't a murder, was it?'

'Flo may need to give the autopsy a second look. I heard some disturbing things while out looking for Hades,'

I waited for the penny to drop. He shrugged.

'I should've known it wouldn't be simple. Make me some more toast.'

Chapter 18

After George had left, I had a quick shower and got dressed. The nasty note from the person claiming to have kidnapped Hades had left me profoundly shocked. Mouse could not know about it. He would not cope with the contents. George could carry on the investigation without us, in theory, but I would get Mouse to investigate Shore Management and Beach Holdings online anyway. Unless they were expert hackers, nobody could follow his trail. He should also go to the vet and trace Hades's original owners. Maybe Hades had returned to them when I chased him away? Apart from that, I intended to follow George's advice and stay well out of the investigation for the time being. I couldn't escape the feeling Gladys held the key to the whole thing even if she didn't realise it. I wanted to show her the letter, but how could I be sure she didn't send it?

I rang Gladys and asked her if she fancied a coffee and a chat at the Vintage. She agreed to meet for elevenses. I hadn't heard anyone call it that for ages. It made me nostalgic for the old days when there were no computers or social media and we did most things in person. I had read somewhere people were suffering an epidemic of loneliness. Did Gladys have any friends left alive? I didn't want to be intrusive, but maybe she would get on with Betty and Irene, if Daphne hadn't poisoned their opinion of her. I would definitely follow up with my plan to invite them all to the Grotty Hovel for tea as soon as we had solved this mystery.

Mouse staggered downstairs before I left, looking rather worse for wear. He had stayed out late at the Christmas party, and I had heard him stumble into the house in the early hours of the morning.

'Did you have fun last night?' I asked.

'Not bad. There were some pretty girls at the party.'

'Why don't you stay at home this morning and do some research on Beach Holdings and Shore Management? I'd love to know who owns them. You could visit the vet's office as well if you feel like it. You'll probably have to put in some sort of request.'

'Okay. I am feeling a teensy bit rough.'

He grinned and showed me a small space between his thumb and forefinger.

'Take your time. I'm seeing Gladys for a coffee at the vintage at eleven. It would be nice if you could make it in by then.'

'It shouldn't take me long to research the companies. I'm an expert at the dark arts now thanks to uni. I'll nip into the vet's on the way to work.'

'Okay. I'll see you there. I'll text you if it's heaving. By the way, don't talk to anyone about the investigation if you can avoid it. George popped in this morning and he's at a delicate stage in the case.'

'I heard him. Did he eat all the bread?'

'No, I saved some for your toast. He's the one who asked you to research Beach Holdings. I'm just the messenger.'

He beamed.

'Thanks. See you later.'

As I made my way to the shop, I realised I had not asked George to describe the woman who worked at Shore Management. I decided to ask him later, after Mouse gave me evidence which I could use as an excuse to swap information. Perhaps I would recognise some of the directors' names. The killer could not hide from us anymore, but sending the note about Hades alerted me to their intention to try. Did they even have him, or had they seen the posters Mouse had put up and chanced their arm? I didn't want to gamble on Hades's life.

I pushed open the door of the shop and stared in at the scene. Weak winter sunshine flooded the space, illuminating the dust particles which danced through the air. The glass fishing floats caught the light and cast multicoloured light on the Christmas decorations. Roz waited for me at the door of the shop, still wrapped in a yellow rain mac, her curly hair bouncing in the breeze.

'I went fishing with Ed last night,' she said. 'I might snatch forty winks on the banquette upstairs if we're not busy first thing.'

'Be my guest. Ghita should be in soon. I expect she cooked her cakes in Surfusion's kitchen, so Rohan will help her carry them across.'

I soon had my hands full with some early customers, both of whom bought silk lamp shades for their mothers. I wrapped them in matching brightly coloured tissue paper, eliciting coos of satisfaction.

'Wow, doesn't the shop look festive?' said Rohan, backing in through the door, carrying three cake tins in his arms. 'Where can I put these? They're orders for Ghita's clients.'

'Just put them under the counter. Is she coming?'

'Yes, I need to help her with the rest of the goodies. She's been on a bake fest most of the night.'

I laughed.

'I think I'm the only member of staff who wasn't up all night, but I didn't get any sleep either.'

'You look tired,' said Rohan. 'Any sign of Hades?'

'No, still missing.'

'How's Mouse taking it?'

'Badly.'

He sighed and left to help Ghita with the rest of the cakes. Soon they had all been placed in their cabinets upstairs. Roz had revived on seeing Ghita, and they were gossiping downstairs when Gladys entered the shop. I waved at her and beckoned her upstairs. She glanced about her, taking in the decorations and the Christmas treasures strewn around the shop with abandon.

'My, it looks so Christmassy,' she said. 'I really should attempt to decorate my flat. I have become very lazy about it the last few years.'

'Do you have any family, Gladys?'

'No. I never married. Cyril was my late autumn romance, but it wasn't to be. All my relatives are dead now.'

'I'm sorry to hear that.'

'I'm used to it. Life goes on.'

She didn't fool me with her stiff upper lip. She wore her loneliness like a cape. My heart bled for her. I made her a pot of tea and a latte for myself, and cut her a slither of Ghita's boozy cherry cake. She popped a piece into her mouth and shut her eyes in bliss.

'I've been talking to my neighbours about Daphne Sand's death,' I said. 'Did you realise she died around the same time Cyril disappeared?'

Her hand hovered in the air with a morsel of cake as she took this in. Then she put it back on her plate, her eyes wide.

'I know now, but as I told you, I had a stay in hospital and became a bit of a hermit around that time. I was shocked to find out she had died. Do you think the deaths are related?'

'It's possible. I'm working on the theory it had something to do with Cyril's house. It's being managed by a property company now.'

'Really? I never thought about it to be honest. I assumed he had sold it. When he deserted me, I stopped going to Keat's Road altogether. The possibility of meeting him or his new girlfriend horrified me.'

'Did you meet Daphne often?'

'No, she didn't like me. She didn't really tolerate anyone, not even her daughter.'

'Oh? I thought they got on well.'

'They did. Until Daphne started talking about leaving her house to the Samaritans. Cyril told me they had a screaming row about it one evening. I'm glad I don't own my flat. Nobody will fight over it when I've gone.'

This rang a bell. Hadn't Violet Kent mentioned a rumour about this at Cyril's funeral? I needed Mouse to confirm my suspicions. It would help if Flo reclassified Daphne's death as suspicious too. If Gladys had been in the hospital when Cyril was murdered, she had a pretty solid alibi. I took the letter George had given me out of my handbag and handed it to her.

'The woman at the property company told George that Cyril sent them this letter authorising them to clear the property and let it out on Airbnb. Do you recognise his signature?'

Gladys took the letter from me and gazed at it for a second.

'This isn't from Cyril,' she said. 'He handwrote all his correspondence. He had beautiful handwriting, you know. Almost like calligraphy. He couldn't use a computer, but he had a phone with text messaging on it.'

She peered at it again.

'And the signature is nothing like his. All you have to do is check the logbook at the Veterans' Club. We always signed in and out together. You'll see it's nothing like this scrawl. It's not even a bad forgery.'

I felt all my Spidey senses tingling and reached for my phone.

'Mouse? I need you to take a photograph of Cyril's signature from the Veterans' Club logbook and send it straight to George. Tell him to compare it to the one on the letter Shore Management got from Beach Holdings. And then come straight here. Gladys has just narrowed down the suspects for us.'

I turned to her again, to find a radiant smile on her face.

'Really? How exciting! I can't believe it.'

'Since you've worked on the case, would you like to join us for Christmas lunch? I can promise you bedlam if that's your sort of thing.'

'Bedlam is my favourite thing.'

'By the way, did Cyril have a cat?'

She put her head on one side.

'How did you know? He had a big mangy black thing he found on the street. That cat used to scratch me every time I tried to stroke it. He ran away just before Cyril disappeared.'

'We found him trapped in a laundry basket when we cleared Cyril's house.'

'He used to like hidey-holes. Maybe he came back looking for Cyril one day and the lid closed on him?'

'Did he have a chip?' I asked.

'I don't think so. He wouldn't let many people near him, but he had a collar.'

'To B love H?'

She smiled.

'Those were our pet names for each other. Bunny and Honey. Do you still have him?'

'It's a long story.'

Chapter 19

I got home to the Grotty Hovel in a great mood and let myself in through an already open front door. I almost shouted about letting Hades escape, but then I remembered he already had. Harry had brought Hades's laundry basket indoors from the shed and leant over it, banging in some tacks. I crept up on him and jumped on his back, kissing his neck. He smelled wrong. I leapt backwards in fright and Nick Fletcher turned around with an amused grin on his face.

'Is that the traditional Seacastle greeting for your brother-in-law?' he said.

I cringed with embarrassment.

'I'm so sorry. I thought you were Harry. You look like him from behind.'

'Same arse, you mean?'

'No. No, I didn't say that. Harry?'

He came out of the kitchen, holding his sides with silent laughter.

'You should've seen your face,' he said. 'It was a picture.'

'Hilarious. I'm so thrilled you're here, Nick. Christmas is going to be brilliant.'

'Thanks, Tan. The photo you sent guilt tripped me, and then I got FOMO as well.'

'Any reasons are good. Have you seen Mouse yet?'

'He's out looking for Hades. I'm fixing up the cat basket. I hear you had a mishap with it.'

He gave me a cheeky grin. If it had been Harry, I'd have punched his arm. Then something white caught my eye. Harry was waving a few sheets of paper in the air.

'What's that?'

'Nick found it under the panel at the bottom of the laundry basket. It makes interesting reading.'

I took it from him and sat at the table with it. I gasped out loud when I got to the second page.

'Holy crap. This is dynamite. Have you told George about it?'

'I thought you'd like the honour.'

'But is it legal?'

'I don't know. It has two witness signatures which George can check,' said Harry. 'I think that's the only requirement for it to be valid. Do you think Gladys knew about the will?'

'Wouldn't she have said something? Why would she let Beach Holdings take over the house? Oh, by the way, I invited her for Christmas too.'

'The more the merrier,' said Harry. 'We have ordered a massive turkey and half a pig ham-wise so we won't have any trouble with supplies. You need to alert the Sargeant Major though, so she cooks enough roasties.'

'I thought we might invite Flo too. She's going to be alone at Christmas too.'

'Brilliant. She's great fun.'

'Who's Flo?' said Nick.

'The local coroner. She's into dead bodies,' said Harry.

'No, she isn't. She's lovely and has great taste in men. She likes them hot, not cold,' I said.

'How do you know?' said Harry.

'Because women talk.'

They both made scared noises and silly faces, like twins. Christmas had arrived early, and the children were already overexcited.

'I'd better call George,' I said.

'Why don't we all go to the Shanty for a drink? We can discuss our theories and I can introduce Nick to Joy and Ryan, our local branch of MI6,' said Harry.

'They're not spies. Don't be silly.'

'If you say so,' said Harry, tapping the side of his nose and making Nick's eye open wide.

Honestly, they were like peas in a pod. Thank goodness they had made up after being estranged for so long. The front door opened and Mouse dragged himself through it, looking defeated.

'No luck?' said Harry.

'Why don't you come to the Shanty with us,' said Nick. 'I found a clue in Hades's basket. It may be crucial to the case.'

'Another detective,' said Mouse. 'Just what we needed.'

While Nick and Harry teased Mouse and persuaded him to come with us, I called George who was still at the office. He agreed to come for a drink and said he'd bring Flo, who had reviewed the notes on the Daphne Sands autopsy. They had been done by Donald Friske, the Brighton pathologist, who stood in for her when she was busy or on holiday.

'Flo thinks you might be right about Daphne,' said George. 'I bet you can't wait to hear it.'

'Wait 'til you focus your peepers on what we found in Hades's basket,' I said. 'I see your bet and I raise you a tenner.'

I put the will into a Ziplock to preserve the prints on it while Harry called a taxi. When it arrived, we all squashed in for our quick trip to the Shanty pub, which teetered near a cliff overlooking Pirate's Harbour. It was by far our favourite watering hole, but not the most accessible one. I gathered from the use of a taxi that Nick and Harry were planning on more than one drink, so I put sensible boots on for following the narrow pathway out of the pub in the darkness. The taxi driver drove us out to the car park nearest to the pub. We booked him to come and take us home just after closing time.

An almost full moon loomed over the wind farm as we make our way along the footpath to the pub.

'Has the cliff got nearer to the pub or am I imagining it?' said Harry.

'I'm trying not to notice,' said Mouse. 'I don't like heights.'

The lights of the pub shone through the windows, giving an enticing golden halo around it. Nick almost knocked his own head off when he failed to duck low enough to enter the low door, a feature of the Shanty. Harry roared with laughter and got a cube of ice from Ryan behind the bar to put on Nick's emerging bruise. We introduced Nick to Ryan and Joy, then made our way with our drinks to the biggest snug at the back of the bar. George and Flo arrived not long after us, and Harry introduced Nick to both of them. Flo had her hair up in a bun tied with a purple ribbon, which matched her velvet jacket. She always looked fabulous and exotic, even in her pathology lab. Nick let Flo slide along the banquette to sit next to Mouse, who indulged in a fragrant hug with one of his favourite people. Then Nick sat next to her before George could react, and Flo blushed crimson when he complimented her on her velvet jacket. I patted the seat next to me and George grunted, but sat without comment.

'Who wants to go first?' I asked.

'I will,' said Flo. 'What I discovered might affect the other contributions.'

'Fair enough,' said Harry. 'We're all ears.'

'I reviewed the coroner's report on the death of Daphne Sands, which was done by Dr Friske after her body was discovered in your house. Before you moved in, I hasten to add.'

Everybody laughed.

'Obviously I can't speak ill of a colleague, but the old codger has got it wrong again.'

George coughed.

'Only joking, boss. Anyway, someone helped Daphne Sands off this moral coil with a blunt object. It's possible… Drum roll please, Mouse.'

He obliged by patting his hands on the table.

'It's possible she was murdered with the same weapon that did for poor Cyril.'

'What she's saying is—' said George.

'We get it,' I said, unable to tolerate him mansplaining to us. 'The same person killed them both.'

'How do you know?' asked Nick, and Flo explained in graphic detail.

His rapt expression told me Flo had scored a bullseye. I removed the will from my handbag and handed it to George.

'And here is the spanner in the works.'

He read it slowly and I struggled not to drum my fingers on the table. Mouse glanced at me and waggled his eyebrows at Nick and Flo. I winked back at him.

'This puts Gladys firmly back in the frame,' said George.

'I would've thought the same if I hadn't chatted with her earlier. She told me she was in the hospital when Cyril vanished. Also, she looked at the letter Beach Holdings claim to have been sent by Cyril and she told me he always handwrote his correspondence and his signature had been forged.'

'Is that why Andrew, sorry Mouse, sent me that photo of the logbook? I didn't have time to read the message.'

'Exactly. So, either someone at Beach Holdings forged the letter to give to Shore Management, or both companies are owned by the same person who forged it themselves.'

Mouse coughed.

'I trawled through the internet and found the names of the directors of Shore Management,' said Mouse.

'Why haven't you told us yet?' said Harry.

'I meant to. I've been so pre-occupied with searching for Hades. Nothing else seemed to matter.'

'Spit it out, boy. Who are they?' said George.

'Some random couple. Jay and Lorna Nuttall. They live—'

'Oh my giddy aunt,' said Harry. 'Mr and Mrs Santa's Elves are double murderers? You couldn't make it up.'

'You know these people?' spluttered George.

'Daphne Sands was Lorna's mother. Gladys told me they had had a shouting match because Daphne had threatened to leave her house to the Samaritans.'

'They killed Daphne for her house? But why did they murder Cyril too?' said Flo, who had stopped staring into Nick's eyes long enough to hear the gist of the conversation.

'I guess he must have seen or heard something he shouldn't have. Poor bloke got caught in the middle,' said Harry.

'They must have realised he had no family and decided that letting out his house would bring them in a steady income,' I said.

'But what proof do we have?' said Mouse. 'We have to establish the ownership of Beach Holdings first and I couldn't find the company on the internet. It's probably a single person, sole trader name.'

'And how do we do that?' said Harry.

'We ask the owner of Shore Management to put us in touch with the owner of Beach Management for a cosy chat down at the station.'

'Lorna Nuttall? Who'd have guessed it?' said Harry.

'Well, that appears to be that,' said George. 'Whose round is it?'

Chapter 20

Everyone in the snug had been excited about breaking the case. For once, George had been grateful for our help. He would get a lot of kudos from his dreaded Superintendent for solving two murder investigations at once. A great Christmas boost for the crime figures. While Mouse went to the toilet, I persuaded George to tell him about the threatening note we had received about Hades, with the white lie that he (George) had forbidden me from telling Mouse about it. The shock written across Mouse's face dissipated when George told Mouse he thought it highly unlikely anyone had really kidnapped Hades. He promised to search high and low at the Nuttall's house anyway, but Mouse insisted on coming with them.

'Anyone else would risk a savaging if they tried to force him into a carrying case.'

I had to admit that he had a point. George sighed, but agreed.

And Flo? I dragged her away from Nick for a joint visit to the ladies.

'What are your intentions towards my future brother-in-law?' I said.

She didn't answer, but gave me a smug smile, which made me laugh.

'Why don't you come to my house for Christmas? Fair warning. Helen and George will be there, but they will be on their best behaviour. I think Nick might like that too.'

She shook her head.

'Spend Christmas with my boss? Hm. It's a nice offer, but I may take a rain check.'

I played my trump card.

'Mouse will be very disappointed if you don't come. He asked me to invite you. He misses you when he's at university, you know.'

Her face softened.

'You know how to make a girl feel bad. Okay. I'll come, as long as I don't have to sit beside George at lunch.'

'It's a deal. I promise I'll sit you between Mouse and Nick.'

'Would you like me to bring anything?'

'How about a nice bottle of red wine? We won't be going teetotal for lunch. You can sleep on the sofa if you're over the limit. Or maybe Mouse will walk to George's house with him and Helen, and let you sleep in his bed?'

'That sounds perfect. I'll look forward to it.'

I lay in bed that night fretting about Hades. Did Lorna have him locked in a shed somewhere? I had all my fingers and toes crossed Hades would be found safe and sound.

I also had nagging doubts about Lorna being the culprit. She had leapt to her mother's defence when she thought I had suggested Daphne had killed Cyril. And she looked nothing like the woman who gave Harry the keys of Cyril's house on clearance day. Lorna's husband had said that she enjoyed dressing up, but Lorna was tall and skinny. The woman who jumped out of the mini was short and stout. Had Lorna paid someone else to give Harry the keys? George would resent it if I interfered in his arrest, but something didn't fit. I couldn't shake the feeling I had missed something.

The next morning, the police van picked up Mouse before daylight had broken. I didn't have to wake him up as he was up and dressed ahead of time. I heard him moving about and crossed my fingers for him. He had made a pot of tea, so I poured myself a cup and sat on the sofa with him until the doorbell rang.

'Do you think Hades is okay?' he said.

'I don't know. I hope so. What reason would she have to hurt him?'

He left with his shoulders slumped. My heart broke for him, but I couldn't concentrate on Hades, because something had lodged in my brain during the night. Something Betty Staples had said. I took out my notebook and re-read all my scrawls. I tried to dismiss the thought, but it wouldn't go away, like an annoying mosquito in a room on a summer's night, buzzing around your head. Finally, I had to get dressed and put on my coat. I crossed the street to Betty Staples's house and knocked on the door. She took a while to answer, and she stood in her dressing gown, without greeting me, a sour look on her face.

'I'm really sorry,' I said. 'It's something you said. I can't get it out of my head. Daphne Sands was murdered, you see, and that changes everything. And—'

Her expression changed in an instant to one of unadulterated excitement. She clapped her hands with glee.

'Murdered? We were right. Have you told Irene?'

'Not yet. I only confirmed it last night. Can you please keep it to yourselves for now? At least until it comes out in the papers?'

'My lips are sealed.'

I doubted that very much, but it was too late to retract.

'When I came looking for our cat, you said a rumour went around about Daphne's death being suspicious.'

'That's right. I did.'

'But you wouldn't tell me where you heard the rumour. It's vital you tell me now. The entire case could rest on it.'

She pursed her lips.

'Well, I'm not one for gossip, but I went to a do at the Veterans' Club once with Irene. They used to have bingo sometimes. During the games, I got talking to that woman who runs the place. She knows everybody's business, she does.'

'Violet Kent?'

'That's her. She's the one who told me about Daphne having a blazing row with her daughter. She said the police should question her. But the coroner told them Daphne fell down the stairs, so I thought she made it up.'

She wiped her hands on her dressing gown.

'Are you saying Lorna killed Daphne?'

'No, I don't think she did. Thank you, Betty. I'll let you get back to bed.'

'But aren't you going to tell me what happened?'

'Not yet. But I promise you can come to tea with Irene and Gladys after Christmas, and I'll give you the complete story.'

I went back across the road and reviewed my notes again. Violet Kent. She had photocopied Mouse's poster about Hades being missing. She had told me about Lorna and Daphne having an argument and had fed a rumour to Betty about Lorna. I thought about our visit to the centre and how over helpful she had been. She would have known all about the veterans' lives and their circumstances. Had she coveted Cyril's house and seen her chance to get it? He would never have suspected her motives for popping in to visit her. With her physique, she was more than capable of burying him among the brambles in Daphne's garden. But why did she bury him there instead of in his own garden? Perhaps it didn't offer the cover of hers. Daphne must have seen something suspicious and confronted her. Perhaps she came home unexpectedly? Violet might have hit her with the same item she used to kill Cyril and staged the accident. I couldn't decide whether to text George. Just because I thought Violet Kent might be the murderer didn't mean Lorna Nuttall was off the hook. I called him anyway.

'What now?'

'I don't think Lorna killed Cyril and Daphne.'

'Neither do I. She just showed me her passport, and she was out of the country when they found Daphne. That's why we didn't interview her last time.'

'I think I know who did it.'

'Is her name Maggie Beach?'

'No.'

'Well, Lorna told us the name of the owner of Beach Holdings. We're on our way to arrest her right now.'

'Maggie Beach? Oh, Harry's note. It must have been Maggie, not Magee.'

'Exactly. Leave it to us, Tan. We're on top of this.'

'Just one thing.'

'What's that? I think her real name is Violet Kent. She's the manageress of the Veterans' Club.'

A deep sigh.

'I'll let you know.'

'By the way, I don't think anybody took Hades. My neighbour, Betty Staples, told me Hades had a habit of absconding for months. If Maggie is actually Violet, she photocopied the lost posters for Mouse. She probably sent me that letter pretending she had kidnapped Hades.'

'I'll tell him. He can come with us to pick her up, just in case.'

But they did not find Hades at Violet Kent's flat, either. So, I had to inform Mouse about Hades's habit of disappearing for months. I couldn't face telling him about my part in it, and a devastated Mouse couldn't understand why Hades had left again. Mouse still searched every day, but Hades had disappeared. Nothing Harry or Nick could do would cheer him up.

Meanwhile, George had interviewed Violet Kent about the murders of Cyril Prout and Daphne Sands. She didn't bother to dispute the facts, admitting she had been on the lookout for an easy way to make money from the veterans. She had found out that Cyril owned a nice terraced house in Kent Road and had chosen him as her victim. Cyril did not suspect her motive when she turned up at his house and let her in. She had murdered him by hitting him with a bludgeon she had found in an antique shop. She referred to Daphne as collateral damage. Daphne had been nosing around the site of Cyril's burial and Violet had got rid of her in case she investigated further. Violet had shown zero remorse for her crimes, only irritation at getting caught. She had been transferred to HMP Bronzefield women's prison where she would spend the holiday, and probably the rest of her life.

George had his double murderer and the kudos that went with it. Typically, the Superintendent had taken all the credit for it. Helen showered George with praise to soften the blow and spent a week in the kitchen cooking for our enlarged family. The last days to Christmas were so busy I felt like shutting the shop instead of dealing with the onrush of clients, but I paid back most of my overdraft and my bank balance finally looked healthier. We shut the shop at midday on Christmas Eve to give us all the time to prepare for the festivities, and Ghita and Roz left to spend Christmas with their families.

We exchanged presents and hugs and I set off for home with Mouse, both of us sad but for different reasons. We both pretended to be jolly on Christmas Eve. We sang carols and drank port and wrapped presents away from prying eyes, but the spectre of Hades haunted our evening.

'Honestly,' said Harry, as I crawled into bed. 'You've got to snap out of it. Hades can look after himself. He's a cat. He'll come back when he wants to.'

'But what if he doesn't want to?'

'Then we'll have to enjoy the love of our family and be glad of our many blessings.'

He kissed me tenderly, and I hid from my troubles in his arms.

'Happy Christmas Eve, my love.'

Chapter 21

I woke early on Christmas morning determined to be positive, but I lay in bed fighting my feelings of misery. Try as I might to avoid the subject, the knowledge of my culpability for Hades's disappearance still affected me. Mouse had not blamed me or let on how much he missed Hades, but I could see it in the slump of his shoulders and the way he kept opening and closing the empty laundry basket in the sitting room. I slipped downstairs to the kitchen and went outside to the garden to take the turkey out of the shed. It needed to be prepped for cooking. I half expected to find Hades there with a smug expression on his face having excavated a large hole in the carcass. But the naked bird sat solidly in its wrapping up on the shelf out of reach, unravaged.

A sob worked its way up my throat and I knew a full-blown wailing fit had ambushed me. I didn't want anyone to hear me cry. The thought of putting a literal damper on Christmas made me ashamed. I decided to sit out in the wind shelter until my sorrow worked itself out. I cut some fatty strips off the ham and put them in a used Ziplock for Herbert. At least I could make his Christmas day happier than mine. I slipped on my fur-lined boots and warmest coat and sneaked out of the front door. The latch clunked on my way out, making me flinch. I hope it didn't wake anyone.

As I walked to the wind shelter, a constant stream of tears leaked down my cheeks. I tried not to sob too loudly in case one of our neighbours came out to see what the racket was and called the Samaritans. They would probably blame Harry and haul him to the clink. I shuffled into the shelter and parked myself against the wall to stem the freezing breeze. The sun had no intention of rising yet and the streetlamps bathed the pebbles in the citrine glow. I stared out at the sea and tried to stop weeping. The spectre of depression still had a powerful hold over me, so I always avoided being unhappy in case it stuck. Maybe that's why I had resisted Harry for so long. My feelings for him terrified me like a tsunami held back by a windbreaker. I wanted to give in and enjoy a happy ever after, but fear always won.

As my sobs subsided and morphed into hiccups, I leaned back and tried to enjoy the sound of the waves filtering through the pebbles as their white foam gleamed yellow in the street lights. I decided to tell the truth about Hades, even if Mouse hated me for it. I took a deep breath and tipped the ham fat onto the ground, hoping Herbert would be the one to find it. No doubt he was ensconced in his nest, dreaming of aiming a stream of faeces at shop windows in the High Street. Then, I caught a movement out of the corner of my eye and swung my legs up on the bench in a fit of panic in case a rat had smelled the bacon and come trundling out of the bushes to investigate. A dark shape emerged from around the corner, a dark shape with a white bib and pointy ears, which leapt upon the scraps with a frenzied hunger. I lowered my legs with caution, letting him finish his meal. Then I whispered.

'Hades? Is that you?'

He looked up at me, licking his mouth, primed to flee. I lowered my hand slowly, so slowly, and scratched him behind one of his soft ears. Instead of scratching me, he leaned into my hand, purring. I slipped my other hand underneath him and levered him up to my lap under the flap of my down coat. His ribs stuck through his fur, but I couldn't see any injuries in the dim light. I wrapped the coat tight against him and felt him go limp. New tears escaped my swollen eyes, and I sat quietly, enjoying the warmth of his body through my clothes. A large grumpy presence disturbed my reverie.

'What on earth are you doing here?' said Harry. 'You frightened the life out of me.'

He didn't sound angry, just worried. Wordlessly, I opened my coat a fraction and pointed at Hades. Harry stifled a chuckle.

'I don't Adam and Eve it,' he said. 'A Christmas miracle.'

A lump came to my throat.

'He's so skinny. And it's all my fault.'

'Don't be silly. It's nobody's fault. How on earth did you get him onto your lap?'

'I don't know. He just let me pick him up.'

'Maybe he missed you.'

I started to cry again.

'Don't fret, darling. He won't be skinny for long in our house. He can eat loads of turkey and ham. Let's go back to the house and snuggle in bed for an hour or two. It's way too early to be up.'

I cradled Hades under my arms and Harry slipped his arm underneath mine to support it. We ambled back to the house. The pain in my heart slipped away like snow sliding off the roof of a house. I could almost hear the thud as it hit the ground. We let ourselves into the Grotty Hovel and gave Hades a couple of packets of his favourite cat food. Then we all went upstairs. I opened Mouse's door and let Hades in. Hades jumped straight onto Mouse's pillow and purred in his ear. Mouse's eyes opened wide with delight.

'Hades? You're home? But how?'

I smiled at him.

'I'll tell you later. Go back to sleep.'

'Happy Christmas, Mum.'

I shut the door, biting my lip. I longed to shout with joy, but I didn't want to embarrass him. Harry waited for me in bed with his arms open. I sunk into their embrace.

'Did you hear?' I asked.

'I heard. Don't cry again. It's supposed to be Merry Christmas, not Teary Christmas.'

I opened my mouth to protest, but he kissed me before I could speak.

'No more talking,' he said.

Thank you for reading my Seacastle Christmas novella. If you have enjoyed this book, please leave me a review on Amazon, Goodreads, Bookbub, or all three. It would be the best Christmas, or anytime, present I could receive as an author.

For those of you who are new to the Seacastle Mystery series, and would like to catch up, please use your phone to read the QR code below. It will take you to book 1, Deadly Return.

The next in the series – **GRAVE REALITY** – (book 7), will be out in early 2025. Pre-order by using your phone to read the QR code below.

Other books

The Seacastle Mysteries - a cosy mystery series set on the south coast of England

Deadly Return (Book 1)

Staying away is hard, but returning may prove fatal. Tanya Bowe, a former investigative journalist, is adjusting to life as an impoverished divorcee in the seaside town of Seacastle. She crosses paths with a long-lost schoolmate, Melanie Conrad, during a house clearance to find stock for her vintage shop. The two women renew their friendship, but their reunion takes a tragic turn when Mel is found lifeless at the foot of the stairs in the same house.

While the police are quick to label Mel's death as an accident, Tanya's gut tells her there's more to the story. Driven by her instincts, she embarks on her own investigation, delving into Mel's mysterious past. As she probes deep into the Conrad family's secrets, Tanya uncovers a complex web of lies and blackmail. But the further she digs, the more intricate the puzzle becomes. As Tanya's determination grows, so does the shadow of danger. Each new revelation brings her closer to a chilling truth. Can she unravel the secrets surrounding Mel's demise before the killer strikes again?

Eternal Forest (Book 2)

What if proving a friend's husband innocent of murder implicates her instead?

Tanya Bowe, an ex-investigative journalist, and divorcee, runs a vintage shop in the coastal town of Seacastle. When her old friend, Lexi Burlington-Smythe borrows the office above the shop as a base for the campaign to create a kelp sanctuary off the coast, Tanya is thrilled with the chance to get involved and make some extra money. Tanya soon gets drawn into the high-stake arguments surrounding the campaign, as tempers are frayed, and her friends, Roz and Ghita favour opposing camps. When a celebrity eco warrior is murdered, the evidence implicates Roz's husband Ed, and Tanya finds her loyalties stretched to breaking point as she struggles to discover the true identity of the murderer.

Fatal Tribute (Book 3)

How do you find the murderer when every act is convincing?

Tanya Bowe, an ex-investigative journalist, agrees to interview the contestants of the National Talent Competition for the local newspaper, but finds herself up to her neck in secrets, sabotage and simmering resentment. The tensions increase when her condescending sister comes to stay next door for the duration of the contest.

Several rising stars on the circuit hope to win the competition, but old stager, Lance Emerald, is not going down without a fight. When Lance is found dead in his dressing room, Tanya is determined to find the murderer, but complex dynamics between the contestants and fraught family relationships make the mystery harder to solve. Can Tanya uncover the truth before another murder takes centre stage?

Toxic Vows (Book 4)

A shotgun marriage can lead to deadly celebrations

Despite her reservations, Tanya Bowe, ex-investigative journalist and local sleuth, feels obliged to plan and attend the wedding of her ex-husband DI George Carter. The atmosphere is less than convivial as underlying tensions bubble to the surface. But when the bride is found dead only hours after the ceremony, the spotlight is firmly turned onto George as the prime suspect. A reluctant Tanya is forced to come to George's aid when his rival, DI Antrim is determined to prove him responsible for her death. She discovers the bride had a lot of dangerous secrets, but so did other guests at the wedding. Did the murderer intend to kill, or have an elaborate plan gone badly wrong?

Mortal Vintage

Does an ancient coven hold the key to solving a murder? Few tears are shed when the unpopular manager of the annual Seacastle Vintage Fair meets a sinister end. But local sleuth Tanya Bowe is thrust into the heart of the investigation when her friend, Grace Wong, finds herself under scrutiny for the murder. When Tanya's investigation uncovers a suspicious death in the same family, all bets are off. She navigates dark undercurrents of greed and betrayal as she uncovers a labyrinth of potential suspects associated with an ancient coven. Nothing is as it seems, and every clue adds extra complications. To solve the case, Tanya must answer one key question. Did someone hate the victim enough to kill her, or was greed the stronger motive?

Last Orders (Book 6)

Has a restaurant critic's scathing review led to his murder?

Local sleuth, Tanya Bowe, attends the long-awaited opening of the Surfusion restaurant. The unexpected arrival of a famous food critic raises the stakes for the owners and increases the buzz of excitement. The evening takes a dark turn when he collapses into his coffee, hours after a scathing review goes live on his blog. The owners are prime suspects for his murder, but Tanya is convinced of their innocence and vows to clear their names. As Tanya digs deeper, what at first seems like an open-and-shut case unravels into a web of intrigue. Is the famous critic even the intended victim of the crime? Tanya Bowe has her work cut out for her as hidden motives lead to simmering tensions among her friends. With time running out and Surfusion's future on the line, can Tanya unmask the culprit before it's too late?

Grave Reality

When death rewrites the script, a reality show takes a fatal detour - Chaos breaks out in the quiet town of Seacastle when the cast and crew of the hit show Sloane Rangers descend upon the town, stirring up drama both on and off the screen. Local sleuth and former investigative reporter, Tanya Bowe, is brought on board as a consultant, tasked with generating buzz for the local and national press. But she quickly uncovers a tangled web of strained relationships and simmering tensions among the cast. When one of the stars is discovered dead on set, she finds herself at the heart of a murder investigation. To complicate matters, the lead detective is her ex-husband, DI George Carter, who's adamant about keeping her out of his investigation. But Tanya isn't one to sit on the sidelines and she's soon up to her neck in controversy. As the case unfolds, a beloved cast member emerges as the prime suspect, sending shockwaves through Seacastle. With everyone playing a part and secrets buried deep, the murderer remains hidden in plain sight. Can Tanya unravel the truth before she becomes the next victim?

Other books by the Author

I write under various pen names in different genres. If you are looking for another mystery, why don't you try **Mortal Mission,** written as Pip Skinner.

Mortal Mission

Will they find life on Mars, or death?

When the science officer for the first crewed mission to Mars dies suddenly, backup Hattie Fredericks gets the coveted place on the crew. But her presence on the Starship provokes suspicion when it coincides with a series of incidents which threaten to derail the mission.

After a near-miss while landing on the planet, the world watches as Hattie and her fellow astronauts struggle to survive. But, worse than the harsh elements on Mars, is their growing realisation that someone, somewhere, is trying to destroy the mission.

When more astronauts die, Hattie doesn't know who to trust. And her only allies are 35 million miles away. As the tension ratchets up, violence and suspicion invade both worlds. If you like science-based sci-fi and a locked-room mystery with a twist, you'll love this book.

The Green Family Saga

Rebel Green – Book 1
Relationships fracture when two families find themselves caught up in the Irish Troubles.
The Green family move to Kilkenny from England in 1969, at the beginning of the conflict in Northern Ireland. They rent a farmhouse on the outskirts of town and make friends with the O'Connor family nearby. Not every member of the family adapts easily to their new life, and their differing approaches lead to misunderstandings and friction. Despite this, the bonds between the family members deepen with time.

Perturbed by the worsening violence in the North threatening to invade their lives, the children make a pact never to let the troubles come between them. But promises can be broken, with tragic consequences for everyone.

Africa Green – Book 2
Will an albino white chimp save its rescuers or get them killed?
Journalist Isabella Green travels to Sierra Leone, a country emerging from civil war, to write an article about a chimp sanctuary. Animals that need saving are her obsession, and she can't resist getting involved with the project, which is on the verge of bankruptcy. She forms a bond with local boy, Ten, and army veteran, Pete, to try to save it. When they rescue a rare albino chimp from a village frequented by a dangerous rebel splinter group, the resulting media interest could save the sanctuary. But the rebel group has not signed the ceasefire. They believe the voodoo power of the white chimp protects them from bullets, and they are determined to take it back so they can storm the capital. When Pete and Ten go missing, only Isabella stands in the rebels' way. Her love

for the chimps unlocks the fighting spirit within her. Can she save the sanctuary or will she die trying?

Fighting Green – Book 3

Liz Green is desperate for a change. The Dot-Com boom is raging in the City of London, and she feels exhausted and out of her depth. Added to that, her long-term boyfriend, Sean O'Connor, is drinking too much and shows signs of going off the rails. Determined to start anew, Liz abandons both Sean and her job, and buys a near-derelict house back in Ireland to renovate.

She moves to Thomastown where she renews old ties and makes new ones, including two lawyers who become rivals for her affection. When Sean's attempt to win her back goes disastrously wrong, Liz finishes with him for good. Finding herself almost penniless, and forced to seek new ways to survive, Liz is torn between making a fresh start and going back to her old loves.
Can Liz make a go of her new life, or will her past become her future?

The Sam Harris Series (written as PJ Skinner)

Set in the late 1980s and through the 1990s, the thrilling Sam Harris Adventure series navigates through the career of a female geologist. Themes such as women working in formerly male domains, and what constitutes a normal existence, are developed in the context of Sam's constant ability to find herself in the middle of an adventure or mystery. Sam's home life provides a contrast to her adventures and feeds her need to escape. Her attachment to an unfaithful boyfriend is the thread running through her romantic life, and her attempts to break free of it provide another side to her character.

The first book in the Sam Harris Series sets the scene for the career of an unwilling heroine, whose bravery and resourcefulness are needed to navigate a series of adventures set in remote sites in Africa and South America. Based loosely on the real-life adventures of the author, the settings and characters are given an authenticity that will connect with readers who enjoy adventure fiction and mysteries set in remote settings with realistic scenarios.

Fool's Gold - Book 1

Newly qualified geologist Sam Harris is a woman in a man's world - overlooked, underpaid but resilient and passionate. Desperate for her first job, and nursing a broken heart, she accepts an offer from notorious entrepreneur Mike Morton, to search for gold deposits in the remote rainforests of Sierramar. With the help of nutty local heiress Gloria Sanchez, she soon settles into life in Calderon, the capital. But when she accidentally uncovers a long-lost clue to a treasure buried deep within the jungle, her journey really begins. Teaming up with geologist Wilson Ortega, historian Alfredo Vargas and the mysterious Don Moises, they venture through the jungle, where she lurches between excitement and insecurity. Yet there is a far graver threat looming; Mike and Gloria discover that one member of the expedition is plotting to seize the fortune for himself and will do anything to get it. Can Sam survive and find the treasure, or will her first adventure be her last?

Hitler's Finger - Book 2

The second book in the Sam Harris Series sees the return of our heroine Sam Harris to Sierramar to help her friend Gloria track down her boyfriend, the historian Alfredo Vargas. Geologist Sam Harris loves getting her hands dirty. So, when she learns that her friend Alfredo has gone missing in Sierramar, she gives her personal life some much needed space and hops on the next plane. But she never expected to be following the trail of a devious Nazi plot nearly 50 years after World War II … Deep in a remote mountain settlement, Sam must uncover the village's dark history. If she cannot reach her friend in time, the Nazi survivors will ensure Alfredo's permanent silence. Can Sam blow the lid on the conspiracy before the Third Reich makes a devastating return?

The Star of Simbako - Book 3

A fabled diamond, a jealous voodoo priestess, disturbing cultural practices. What might go wrong? The third book in the Sam Harris Series sees Sam Harris on her first contract to West Africa to Simbako, a land of tribal kingdoms and voodoo. Nursing a broken heart, Sam Harris goes to Simbako to work in the diamond fields of Fona. She is soon involved with a cast of characters who are starring in their own soap opera, a dangerous mix of superstition, cultural practices, and ignorance (mostly her own). Add a love triangle and a jealous woman who wants her dead and Sam is in trouble again. Where is the Star of Simbako? Is Sam going to survive the chaos?

The Pink Elephants - Book 4
Sam gets a call in the middle of the night that takes her to the Masaibu project in Lumbono, Africa. The project is collapsing under the weight of corruption and chicanery engendered by management, both in country and back on the main company board. Sam has to navigate murky waters to get it back on course, not helped by interference from people who want her to fail. When poachers invade the elephant sanctuary next door, her problems multiply. Can Sam protect the elephants and save the project or will she have to choose?

The Bonita Protocol - Book 5
An erratic boss. Suspicious results. Stock market shenanigans. Can Sam Harris expose the scam before they silence her? It's 1996. Geologist Sam Harris has been around the block, but she's prone to nostalgia, so she snatches the chance to work in Sierramar, her old stomping ground. But she never expected to be working for a company that is breaking all the rules. When the analysis results from drill samples are suspiciously high, Sam makes a decision that puts her life in peril. Can she blow the lid on the conspiracy before they shut her up for good?

Digging Deeper - Book 6

A feisty geologist working in the diamond fields of West Africa is kidnapped by rebels. Can she survive the ordeal, or will this adventure be her last? It's 1998. Geologist Sam Harris is desperate for money, so she takes a job in a tinpot mining company working in war-torn Tamazia. But she never expected to be kidnapped by blood thirsty rebels.

Working in Gemsite would never be easy with its culture of misogyny and corruption. Her boss, the notorious Adrian Black is engaged in a game of cat and mouse with the government over taxation. Just when Sam makes a breakthrough, the camp is overrun by rebels and Sam is taken captive. Will anyone bother to rescue her, and will she still be alive if they do?

Concrete Jungle - Book 7 (series end)

Armed with an MBA, Sam Harris is storming the City - But has she swapped one jungle for another?

Forging a new career would never be easy, and Sam discovers she has not escaped from the culture of misogyny and corruption that blighted her field career.

When her past is revealed, she finally achieves the acceptance she has always craved, but being one of the boys is not the panacea she expected. The death of a new friend presents her with the stark choice of compromising her principals to keep her new position, or exposing the truth behind the façade. Will she finally get what she wants or was it all a mirage?

Box Sets

Sam Harris Adventure Box Set Book 2-4
Sam Harris Adventure Box Set Book 5-7
Sam Harris Adventure Box Set Books 2-7

Connect with the Author

About the Author

I write under several pen names and in various genres: PJ Skinner (Travel Adventures and Cozy/Cosy Mystery), Pip Skinner (Sci-Fi), Kate Foley (Irish contemporary), and Jessica Parkin (children's illustrated books).

I moved to the south coast of England just before the Covid pandemic and after finishing my trilogy, The Green Family Saga, I planned the Seacastle Mysteries. I have always been a massive fan of crime and mystery and I guess it was inevitable I would turn my hand to a mystery series eventually.

Before I wrote novels, I spent 30 years working as an exploration geologist, managing remote sites and doing due diligence on projects in over thirty countries. During this time, I collected the tall tales and real-life experiences which inspired the Sam Harris Adventure Series, chronicling the adventures of a female geologist as a pioneer in a hitherto exclusively male world.

I worked in many countries in South America and Africa in remote, strange, and often dangerous places, and loved every minute, despite encountering my fair share of misogyny and other perils. The Sam Harris Adventure Series is for lovers of intelligent adventure thrillers happening just before the time of mobile phones and the internet. It has a unique viewpoint provided by Sam, a female interloper in a male world, as she struggles with alien cultures and failed relationships.

My childhood in Ireland inspired me to write the Green Family Saga (as Kate Foley), which follows the fortunes of an English family who move to Ireland just before the start of the troubles.

I have also written a mystery on Mars, Mortal Mission, inspired by my fascination with all things celestial. It is a science-based murder mystery, think The Martian with fewer potatoes and more bodies.

Follow me on Amazon to get informed of my new releases. Just put PJ Skinner into the search box on Amazon and then click on the follow button on my author page.

Please subscribe to my Seacastle Mysteries Newsletter for updates and offers by using this QR code

You can also use the QR code below to get to my website for updates and to buy paperbacks direct from me.

You can also follow me on Twitter, Instagram, TikTok, or on Facebook @pjskinnerauthor

Printed in Great Britain
by Amazon